"I'm not who I am."

Maggie's tone was insistent. "Why don't you believe me?"

"Are you sure you know what you're saying?" Logan asked.

"Yes. Three months ago, I was riding along with my client, wishing I had that kind of money, that kind of life—"

"Wait a minute. Didn't I read that Madeline Van Waltonscot had been in a serious car accident that had killed her passenger?"

"I'm sure you did, because it's true. Sort of . . ." Maggie saw Logan frown. Before he could say anything, she continued. "Technically, both the passenger—Maggie Morgan—and the heiress died. But Madeline Van Waltonscot's body was revived. And after two months in a coma, I woke up . . . and that body was mine!"

Dear Reader,

We're thrilled that you're spending your summer with Strummel Investigations. I know you'll agree that this P.I. firm is one unique family business!

Victoria Pade brings us brother Logan's story this month—and it's slightly "out of this world"! Logan's seen some bizarre cases, but nothing quite as mind-blowing as Maggie Morgan's claim that her soul has taken up residence in another woman's body!

Victoria and I hope you've enjoyed all the Strummel Investigations stories. In case you missed any, there's still a chance to order the earlier titles. See the ad in the back pages.

Enjoy the rest of your summer!

Regards,

Debra Matteucci
Senior Editor & Editorial Coordinator
Harlequin
300 E. 42nd St.
New York, NY 10017

Victoria Pade

THE CASE OF THE ACCIDENTAL HEIRESS

Harlequin Books

TORONTO • NEW YORK • LONDON
AMSTERDAM • PARIS • SYDNEY • HAMBURG
STOCKHOLM • ATHENS • TOKYO • MILAN
MADRID • WARSAW • BUDAPEST • AUCKLAND

ISBN 0-373-16594-3

THE CASE OF THE ACCIDENTAL HEIRESS

Copyright © 1995 by Victoria Pade.

Printed in U.S.A.

Prologue

Well, if this wasn't the weirdest thing.

Maggie Morgan didn't know where she was.

Or how she'd gotten there.

Or why she felt so strange.

Light-headed. Dizzy.

And tired. She was really tired. More tired than she'd ever been in her life. Even moving her head took so great an effort she could only do it slowly, as if she were held down by a great weight, only the weight was all around her....

Sleep. I must need sleep. I must be exhausted.

Or maybe she already was asleep.

Maybe that's why everything was so dark.

But she didn't feel as if she were sleeping; she felt wide awake. And she was standing up. Sort of. Actually, she seemed to be floating.

Floating?

How could she be awake and floating and feeling weighted all at the same time? It must be a dream.

A dream about a tunnel, that was it. She had the sense that she was in a tunnel. A dark tunnel. And there, at the other end, was a light.

The light at the end of the tunnel.

Oh, good. She was dreaming in clichés. What was next? Would she be in a cloud's silver lining? Or putting the cart before the horse? Or out of her league?

Nope, she was already out of her league because she suddenly realized that right beside her was Madeline Van Waltonscot, the heiress for whom she was working.

Now that was weird.

Sharing the daytime with the heiress was bad enough, sharing a dream made Maggie a glutton for punishment.

Except that then she remembered something that made her sure she wasn't having a dream.

They'd been in Madeline Van Waltonscot's car. Miss Van Waltonscot had been driving. Much, much too fast. And Maggie had been thinking about how afraid she was, about the possibility that the heiress was scaring her just for kicks.

Maggie had been thinking that if she were in Madeline Van Waltonscot's shoes, she wouldn't need such cheap thrills. Would that she *were* in Madeline Van Waltonscot's shoes!

So where was the car? They might be in a long, dark tunnel, but they weren't driving through it in the heiress's fancy sports car.

Maggie tried to ask, to call out her client's name. But she couldn't make a sound.

Yet she'd somehow gotten the other woman's attention because the heiress looked at her, turning her head in slow motion and raising her arm to point downward.

Maggie followed the direction and saw that wherever they were, they had a bird's-eye view into a hospital emergency room, overlooking two tables. And two teams of doctors and nurses gathered around each of them, their frantic ministrations obscuring the patients they attended.

Strange, Maggie thought in a removed sort of way, much more interested in what was going on up here than down there.

She heard one of the doctors say, "This one's gone. There's no more we can do," and watched as that group began to disperse. But before they did, a nurse pulled a sheet completely over whoever was on that table.

Maybe she and her client had gone to the movies, Maggie thought, because the drama that was playing below them seemed more like cinema than anything real.

"We're losing this one, too!" a woman doctor said from the head of the other table.

Only mildly interested, Maggie watched as that team stepped back and the doctor held some sort of paddles to the chest of the patient.

Madeline Van Waltonscot! That patient was Madeline Van Waltonscot!

But how could that be? The heiress was right there next to her. Again Maggie tried to speak, to ask what was going on, but still no words would come.

Then suddenly the light at the other end of the tunnel got so bright that she stopped being curious about anything. Instead she felt compelled to turn away from the scene below, to face the light no matter how much effort it took.

And it did take some effort. A lot of it.

But once she'd managed it, she was drawn toward the light and the exquisite warmth coming from it. To the incredible sense of love and acceptance. To the most wonderful feeling . . .

Madeline Van Waltonscot was up ahead now, moving in the direction of the light, floating there with none of the difficulty Maggie was having.

Maggie just couldn't seem to budge. Not at all. Not even in that slow, thick way she had before.

Hey! Cut me loose here! I want to go, too! she tried to call out.

But again no sound came, and this time her client didn't even acknowledge her attempt. She just went on without Maggie, reaching the light and disappearing into it in a blinding flash that made the light swell out to touch Maggie with a serenity more complete than she'd ever known.

And then it was gone.

And she was alone in the darkness.

Terrific. Leave it to me to miss the boat. Or the last bus out of here. Now what?

As if in answer to her thought, she felt a tug that brought her around in the direction she'd been before, and once more she was looking into the hospital emergency room.

The woman doctor was again applying those paddles to the patient. "Stand clear!" she shouted.

Everyone did. But when the jolt lifted Madeline Van Waltonscot's body off the table, Maggie felt it.

Did those things ricochet?

"Once more," she heard the doctor say.

You're too late, Maggie tried to tell them.

But another shock rocked Madeline Van Waltonscot's body, and Maggie's, too.

Then the air around her became compressed and started to suck her down into the emergency room.

No, wait! Somebody's making a mistake! A huge mistake! Pay attention! This can't be right! You've got the wrong girl....

Though she tried clumsily to resist, she was pulled down through the darkness. Down into the hospital's ugly electric light. Down into the noise and commotion. Down into the body the doctor was working so hard to save.

And all she could think was, *Oh boy, somebody fouled up big time.*

Then she heard herself groan in a voice that didn't belong to her.

Chapter One

Strummel Investigations.

She looked from the business card in her hand to the sign in front of the two-story red-brick house with its steep roof and big front porch, then back to the card.

This was the place, all right. Although a quaint old home with a carriage house out back and huge elm and oak trees surrounding it didn't seem a likely site for a private investigator's office.

But then she knew better than anyone that appearances could be deceiving.

She walked up to the front door, which was open to let in the crisp autumn air through the screen. The cozy furniture in the living room and the lovely deacon's bench beside the stairs told her that this place was someone's home as well as office. So rather than going in, she rang the doorbell.

"Just a second," a deep male voice called from what sounded like the kitchen, and she felt slightly better just hearing it. Surely the owner of a voice like that could handle anything.

But could he *believe* anything?

When he appeared from down the hall, the thought that flickered through her mind at that first sight of him was that he would definitely be able to handle anything.

The man was big—a full six feet three inches if her guess was right. He had a solid, muscular build, most evident in the shoulders that were so broad they seemed to fill the whole width of the hallway. Or at least they were wide enough to block her view.

So she raised her gaze from there to his face.

And what she found at that higher elevation took her breath away.

He was drop-dead gorgeous.

His hair was the dark brown color of unsweetened chocolate. His face was all sharp planes carved at just the right angles to leave hollowed cheeks and a razor-edged jaw.

His nose was slightly long but so streamlined it looked as if a classical Greek master had fashioned it, along with his mouth, with its slightly full bottom lip and corners that curled up even now when his expression was sober, curious and businesslike. It was very sexy. And the eyes that took her in from beneath the square forehead were a smoldering heather gray.

This guy shouldn't be a real-life private investigator, she thought, *he should be one on television or in the movies.*

As he neared the door, she remembered why she was there—and it wasn't to gawk at the man. "I need to speak to an investigator, if I could," she said politely. "I'm—"

"I know who you are. You're Madeline Van Waltonscot," he said, tersely cutting her off. When she looked at him again, she found that his male-model features had suddenly hardened into a very stern and off-putting expression.

She swallowed with some difficulty. "Yes, well—"

"You're barking up the wrong tree here," he went on in more of that very unfriendly way. "Strummel Investigations doesn't do party security, bodyguarding, chauffeuring or shopping accompaniment and package carrying."

She tried not to feel too intimidated. It wasn't easy. He was an imposing man. "I don't want to hire someone for any of those things. I need an investigation done."

He didn't respond, but merely stared daggers at her through the screen, wearing a very suspicious look.

She ignored his bad manners and forged on. "Please. Could we just talk?"

He studied her for a moment more before he finally pushed open the screen. It was the only concession he made. He didn't ask her in but merely stood aside, his long arm stretched out to hold the door, one thick eyebrow raised in what she surmised to be some sort of warning.

You'd better be on your best behavior, was what she interpreted that arched brow to mean, and she couldn't help wondering if this man and Madeline Van Waltonscot had had previous—and unpleasant—dealings.

But there was something about his attitude that said he only recognized who she was, not that they were actually acquainted, though he probably knew enough about Madeline Van Waltonscot to cause that attitude.

She didn't hold it against him.

Once she was inside, he turned and walked back the way he'd come, still without saying anything.

She followed his lead, taking a gander at the most terrific rear end she'd ever seen.

That's what you get for not letting the lady go first, she thought, unabashedly enjoying the view of that khaki-clad backside.

He went into what was obviously the office of Strummel Investigations—a large open room complete with three desks, a computer, several filing cabinets and only a single fern hanging in the corner to ease the starkness of the work environment.

He sat behind one of the desks and motioned her to the chair in front of it.

"Are you Mr. Strummel?" she ventured as she perched on the edge of the seat, raising the card she still held in her hand as a reference.

"I'm one of them. Logan."

"Should I call you Mr. Strummel or—"

"Just Logan will be fine. We aren't formal around here."

But he was very curt. She tried to ignore that, too.

"What is it you need investigated?" he asked. Demanded, actually, and in a challenging tone.

"It's very complicated, and before I tell you I have to know that it'll be held in the strictest confidence," she answered, also trying not to notice the intense scrutiny of those gray eyes.

"Absolutely," he assured with a tiny note of annoyance that she even needed to question his discretion.

"I also hope you're an open-minded person," she hedged. "This will be very hard for you to believe. Almost impossible, in fact. To tell you the truth, I'm having a lot of trouble grasping it myself." Another of the hard swallows. "But I'm in the most incredible predicament." The understatement made her laugh just a little, but it was mirthless and uncomfortable.

He didn't crack a smile to put her more at ease. He just went on staring at her without giving any encouragement, like a psychiatrist watching her over long, thick fingers pressed together at the tips.

He wore a cream-colored shirt with the sleeves rolled to just below elbows that were braced on the chair arms, revealing thick wrists and hands large enough to easily palm a basketball. They looked very strong, very powerful, very capable. They looked like good hands in which to place her problems.

"Is there a specific reason you don't...like me?" she heard herself ask.

"I don't really know you except by sight, Ms. Van Waltonscot. Not that you'd remember if we had, but we've never actually been introduced."

That confirmed her earlier assumption. And it was a relief. Less close encounters meant less to overcome. "Please call me Maddie," she told him congenially.

"Maddie?" he repeated with disbelief.

"I'm not who you think I am. Well, of course I am—on the outside. But not on the inside."

He looked dubious, to say the least. But then what else could he be?

She rushed on. "Have you ever heard the saying, be careful what you wish for because you might get it?"

He only arched another brow at her.

"Well, it seems that's what's happened to me. Three months ago I was riding in Madeline Van Waltonscot's car—"

"In *your* car, you mean."

"Just bear with me." She took a breath and blew it out, struggling for the courage to go through with this. "I was redecorating Miss Van Waltonscot's guest house. Actually, I worked for a design firm that she'd hired and no one liked her so, being the new kid on the block, I got the job of trying to please her."

"*You* were working for Madeline Van Waltonscot?"

"I told you, I'm not who I am."

"Uh-huh."

She pretended not to notice his patronizing tone and went on.

"Miss Van Waltonscot insisted I spend an entire day with her so I could get the right feel for her tastes and style. It was a long day, I can tell you. And a long night and into the next morning. She dragged me around until 3:00 a.m., all the while expecting me to be seen and not heard while she talked and talked and talked. A mile a minute. Almost as fast as she drove."

"Are you sure you know what you're saying?" he asked.

She had drifted a little, remembering that night much, much too vividly. But his voice brought her back.

"Yes, I know what I'm saying. Anyway, on that drive home she gave me this lecture about what she wanted in the way of redecorating, which was more elaborate than anything I'd ever done before, and how much she was willing to spend, which was more than what my entire college education cost. I was riding along, scared half-silly because she was driving thirty miles over the speed limit, and only half listening to her by then while my mind wandered. I was wishing I had that kind of money, that kind of life—"

"Three months ago—didn't I read that you had been in a serious car accident that had killed your passenger?"

"I'm sure you did because it's true. Sort of, anyway. What you couldn't have read, because no one but me knows, is that the passenger wasn't exactly killed. Madeline Van Waltonscot was."

A frown put twin lines between those agile eyebrows of his, but before he could say anything she continued her story.

"Technically, both the passenger—Maggie Morgan—and the heiress died in the emergency room. But Madeline Van Waltonscot's body was revived. And after two months in a coma, when I woke up... that body was mine."

"Come on!"

"And not only have I, plain old Maggie Morgan, found myself in someone else's body, in someone else's life, but in someone else's trouble, too."

He laughed. A loud, barrel-deep hoot of a laugh.

She didn't take offense. She knew how preposterous this all sounded. "I told you it was hard to believe."

"Hard to believe? You have to be kidding."

In spite of his undisguised skepticism, she felt relieved to have gotten the whole story off her chest for the first time and she sank back into the chair. "I wish I *were* kidding," she assured him.

She didn't know what it was about her last statement that made him take a second look at her, but he did. A closer look.

Then he stood.

She half expected him to grab her by the scruff of her neck and throw her out. But he merely said, "Will you excuse me for a minute?" and left the office.

She sat up straighter, all the way back in the seat now, and wondered where he'd gone. Was he calling someone to come and take her away because he thought she was crazy?

Of course he thought she was crazy. What else could he think after hearing her say she wasn't really Madeline Van Waltonscot, but Maggie Morgan, somehow lost from her own body and now occupying that of an heiress to a national grocery-store chain?

Even *she* sometimes thought she'd gone crazy. Every morning she rushed out of bed to the mirror to see if she was herself again.

But every morning it was Madeline Van Waltonscot's face that looked back at her.

Maddie—she had persuaded everyone she'd encountered since awakening to call her that.

She certainly couldn't ask to be called Maggie; she'd have been locked up from the start. But Maddie sounded enough like Maggie that she at least felt more herself. Or at least a little closer to herself. Actually, after three weeks, she was beginning to think of herself as Maddie.

Unfortunately the other problems she'd found herself in hadn't been so easily solved.

Which was why she was there.

But where had that investigator gone for so long? she wondered.

Maybe she shouldn't have come. Maybe she shouldn't have risked telling anyone. Maybe she should have just gone on as she had since awakening from that coma—trying to bluff her way through another woman's life, hoping this great cosmic joke might end and she might turn back into herself again.

And maybe Logan Strummel really was off calling the authorities—someone who would cause her even more problems.

She stood and headed for the door, running face first into the big, powerfully muscled wall of Mr. Strummel's chest as he finally returned.

His reflexes were quick—those massive hands of his snaked out to her arms and steadied her on her feet as she bounced back from his body, leaving her oddly aware of just how much man he was.

"Maybe this wasn't such a good idea," she said in a hurry.

"I just made a pot of coffee. You might as well stay and have a cup. You haven't told me yet what it is you want investigated."

The thought flashed through her mind that he was stalling until the guys in the white coats could come to drag her away.

But his hands were still at her arms, and they were gentle, not detaining her, just bolstering her. And sending an electrical current shooting from him to her in a strange, disconcertingly pleasant way.

Somehow it left her with an inclination to trust him. Even more than she already had.

And when she glanced up at his handsome face and found an absence of his previous disdain, she was convinced not to run.

Of course she didn't see acceptance and belief in his eyes, either, but at least he seemed to be cutting her a little slack. And he was curious; that much she could tell for sure.

"Okay," she answered. "If you give me your word you haven't called someone to cart me off to the loony bin."

"Madeline Van Waltonscot does not say things like 'loony bin,'" he pointed out as if she were blowing an impersonation.

"Madeline Van Waltonscot has gone off to the great beyond," she countered in a confidential aside as if he might have forgotten.

"And left Maddie behind," he confirmed with just a tinge of facetiousness.

"Fusion. Maggie plus Madeline equals Maddie."

"You."

"Me."

After another moment he released his hold on her arms. "Coffee's probably ready. Will we need three cups?"

Ah, so he had a sense of humor. Good. She smiled. "No, that's okay, I'll be drinking for the two of us."

"What do you think about coming into the kitchen to fix it? And while we're at it you can tell me who Maggie Morgan is . . . or was."

"Ah, a quiz."

"Any problem with that?"

"Nope."

As she followed him out of the office she seized the subject, trying to concentrate on that, rather than stealing another glance at his derriere.

"I was born Margaret Marie Morgan to a Kansas minister, Curtis Morgan, and his wife Dinah. I was an only child, and both my parents passed away within two months of each other a few years ago. I didn't have any other family, and when the last of my friends married and moved away, I decided to make a change myself. So just after Christmas I came to Denver, was hired by Designs Unlimited and was just getting acquainted with some new people when the accident happened."

"And voilà! You're a new woman."

"This isn't any easier for me to believe than for you," she said over her first sip of coffee. "If there was anything I could do to change back into myself, I would. But since there doesn't seem to be, I'll do whatever it takes to prove to you that although I may be Madeline Van Waltonscot on the outside, I'm not on the inside."

"And why do you need an investigator?"

"Some worrisome things have been happening that I don't understand, and so I decided to hire someone who might be able to help me figure it out. Your business card was in the purse the hospital returned to me when I was released. I've never done something like hire a private investigator before, and that seemed as good a recommendation as any."

She climbed onto a stool at the island counter, feeling at home in the cozy atmosphere of the kitchen, with its oak cupboards, aged red-brick walls and cream-and-tan marble countertops.

The island held well-used cutting boards on either side of a five-burner stove, and overhead was a cast-iron cache rack lined with copper pots and pans. "You must like to cook," she observed as he settled onto a stool just around the corner of the counter.

"I grew up here—this is our family home. But it belongs to my older brother and his soon-to-be-wife now. My place is out back, above the garage."

She nodded. "The carriage house. I noticed it when I got here."

He didn't seem to want to talk about himself. Instead he took a drink of his coffee and said, "Tell me what 'worrisome' things have been happening."

"It started the second day I was out of the coma. A rough-looking man with a bent nose came to my hospital room. Of course I didn't know who he was, but he seemed to know me—more like he worked for me...for Madeline Van Waltonscot.

"All Bent Nose said was that he'd been checking on me since the accident and he was glad I'd made it. And that I should rest assured he would take up where he'd left off so I'd get my money's worth. Then he sort of slipped out secretively—you know, looking both ways before he would actually go out into the hall."

"Cryptic maybe, but worrisome? He could have been hired to do anything, gardening, plumbing."

"But that's not all. Since then I've received two typed notes without a greeting, signature or return address."

"You're assuming it's Bent Nose?"

Maddie took the notes out of her pantsuit pocket and handed them across the counter. "The first one says, 'Just to let you know—have begun warnings again as planned,' and the other says, 'Have planted evidence against the wife.'"

She paused a moment to let him take a look.

When he gave them back she went on. "Then, yesterday morning when I came out of the shower, there was a message on the answering machine. But it wasn't Bent Nose. It was a different man's voice—more educated, more refined, less smug. He didn't identify himself, either, but he was very angry and upset. He said he was sorry I'd survived to start my nasty tricks again—me being Madeline Van Waltonscot."

"Did he threaten you?"

"No, but he sounded dangerously angry. And the thing is, it's bad enough that I'm in a position to have to live the everyday life of another person. Madeline Van Waltonscot lives so differently from what I've ever known that I might as well be on Mars. And believe me, it isn't nearly as great as I imagined it would be riding in that car with her that night. But it also looks as if she was involved in something unsavory or unethical or..."

"Illegal," he supplied.

"Something that seems intended to hurt someone in some way. Only now it isn't Madeline Van Waltonscot who's involved. It's me."

His eyes narrowed at her, and his expression hardened again the way it had at the front door before he'd let her in. "I see. So what's really going on here is that you got into something bigger and worse than you expected and want me to get you out of it. And in order to appear innocent, you'd like me to believe you're not Madeline Van Waltonscot, but instead the poor woman who died in that accident. This is a pretty elaborate, not to mention despicable, con to garner some help."

"No, that's not it! Yes, I do need help. I need someone—you—to find out what's going on and stop it or fix whatever damage has been done if you can, or... I don't know... Just let me know what's going on. But I'm not conning you."

He stared at her once more, that terrific mouth of his relaying an unpleasant sneer of disgust.

Clearly he believed the worst of her. But she knew no one else was going to accept her fantastic tale, so she opted for pleading her case with him rather than starting from scratch with someone new.

"You can investigate anything you want to help you see that I really am Maggie Morgan on the inside. You can ask me intimate details of my past and then look into them to have them confirmed. You can do anything it takes to convince yourself that I'm not making this up—no matter how bizarre it sounds. In fact, I'd welcome it. Maybe if you do some initial investigating of me—Maggie Morgan—you'll even come across my things. There were pictures of my parents, keepsakes, mementos, which I'd like to have back.''

Logan Strummel regarded Maddie thoughtfully for a moment. "What's your medical condition since the accident?''

She knew what he was thinking. "I'm fine. My physical injuries healed while I was in the coma. And mentally,'' she added wryly, "I'm as good as can be expected of someone who woke up to find herself stuck in someone else's body, forced to live someone else's life. But I'll arrange with the hospital and the doctors for you to check all the medical records if that will help you believe me.''

She was finished with her coffee and tired of sitting beneath his scrutiny, so she picked up her mug, took it to the sink, rinsed it and left it there before returning to the stool.

For the second time she noticed a slight change in his expression, and while it didn't hold any more belief than before, at least he wasn't looking at her as if she were the lowest life form on earth.

"I hope you understand that I'll dig pretty deep into this story you've told me. And you should also know that until a week ago I was a Denver cop, so if you're doing something illegal, I'll not only turn you in, I'll make damn sure you're prosecuted.''

She flinched slightly at that. ''I don't know if what's going on is illegal or not. If that's the case, it's Madeline Van Waltonscot's doing, not mine.''

His only answer was a challenging raise of his eyebrows.

Maddie thought about the risk she was running, but it didn't take long for her to make a decision. ''I can't just let this slide when it seems as if some wrong is being done. I guess I'll have to chance it.''

She looked back at the investigator's handsome face, wishing she weren't so aware of just how attractive he was, of even the small details of his striking features. After all, he was a man who could potentially do her more harm than good.

But gorgeous or not, perilous or not, this was something she had to do.

''Are you saying you'll take the case?'' she asked.

''Right here and now? No. First I'm checking out Maggie Morgan and those medical records. When I've done that I'll think it over and let you know.''

''Soon?''

''This is Friday. I'll decide over the weekend and let you know on Monday.''

She nodded, accepting his answer because she had no other choice, although she'd have rather he'd been able to start work immediately. ''I'll come back here Monday then, in the afternoon, and you can tell me if you'll help me. Would that be okay?''

''Fine.''

''What if something bad comes up in the meantime? Should I just call the police?''

"Tell the police this story and you'll be in the psych ward faster than you can say Maggie Morgan." He pointed his blunt chin toward her purse where it lay on the counter. "Do you have that business card you waved around before?"

She found it and gave it to him.

He turned it over and wrote on it, then handed it back. "That's my private phone number. If it's an emergency you can use it. If something else 'worrisome' happens but it isn't urgent, you can call the office number and leave a message."

She slipped the card into her purse again, thanking him as she stood to go. "I know you don't believe me and that you probably think it's my mind I've lost instead of my body, but it helps just to have told someone all of this. I'll go by the hospital on my way home and make sure they know to release the records to you. And if there's anything else you need . . ."

"I'll find you."

"I'll see you in a couple of days then," she said by way of an exit line.

But for some reason she didn't quite understand, when it came down to it, she wasn't anxious to leave.

Maybe because for the first time since waking from that coma she'd actually been in an environment that was more what she was used to.

Or maybe it had to do with finally sharing the burden of this incredible thing that had happened to her, even to someone who wasn't altogether responsive, and hating that now she'd have to return to the charade.

Or maybe it had to do with Logan Strummel himself.

Chapter Two

When Logan's alarm went off at seven o'clock Monday morning, he woke amid library books and sheets of paper with notes written on them.

The notes were his own, taken from phone calls and computer checks regarding Maggie Morgan. The library books were about near-death experiences.

And he'd been up most of the night before going through every shred of information he'd gathered.

Now he was tired and wondering if he'd lost *his* mind to even be considering taking this case. Especially when he just plain didn't believe Madeline Van Waltonscot's story.

Not that he was convinced she was out and out lying, though that was one of two possibilities more likely than dying and coming back in someone else's body. But if she wasn't pulling some sort of scam or con, he thought she was probably suffering a mental breakdown.

The doctors he'd spoken to at the hospital assured him they believed her to be mentally sound following a brief period of disorientation just after awakening from the coma. But doctors didn't always know everything. She could have hidden what she'd called her predicament so as not to be thought crazy. Logan didn't think he could rule out the possibility that Madeline Van Waltonscot had a deep-seated guilt that had manifested itself in adopting the identity of the woman she had killed in that accident.

Logan sat up in bed and gathered the debris of his research, wondering if he should have been reading psychology books instead.

Nevertheless, what kind of trouble had Madeline Van Waltonscot gotten into? Why would she, of all people, need some tough guy to do what sounded like dirty work on her behalf?

Back to the first possibility—was she lying? Perhaps she'd made up this whole fantastic body-exchange story as a cover, albeit a pretty strange one. Such a story might go a long way in convincing a judge and jury to accept a plea of insanity. Which would mean she was trying to enlist him in the scam.

That notion made him all the more intent on not letting her get away with whatever it was she had up her sleeve.

Maybe things would change the longer he was away from the police force, but only being a week out of it, he was still thinking like a cop. Even the hint of wrongdoing was something he couldn't turn his back on.

So, was he going to take the case to expose her?

Maybe.

But what really had him hooked was curiosity. There was a lot in what Madeline Van Waltonscot said and did that sparked his interest.

Among other things, she had sparked—

But he pushed those other things out of his mind, concentrating instead on what had been niggling him since their meeting: his difficulty believing what he'd seen with his own eyes—the change in the Madeline Van Waltonscot he knew.

As a cop he'd pulled parade and dignitary duty more often than he'd liked. Acting as security for high-society events wasn't why he'd become a police officer. Even though private security performed the bulk of those jobs, whenever the mayor or the governor or a visiting high-profiler was in attendance, local law enforcement usually put a few men on the scene just in case. And Logan's stints at it had given him an up-close and personal view, not only of people *like* Madeline Van Waltonscot, but of Madeline Van Waltonscot herself.

He wasn't a fan of the rich and famous. In fact, close contact with them had turned him off completely. They weren't people he would ever choose to be around. But of all the nose-in-the-air types, Madeline Van Waltonscot was the worst.

The queen of snobs. Snide, shrewish, supercilious, demanding, demeaning and completely insufferable. She was well-known not only as one of the richest women around, but also as the rudest and most pretentious. In short, the woman was one hundred and fifty percent *bitch*.

So where had all that gone? And how could anyone so completely and successfully submerge what seemed to be her true nature? He'd found himself wondering if the woman sitting across from him really was Madeline Van Waltonscot.

How good a judge was he, anyway? He hadn't had a lot to do with her on the few occasions when she'd attended the same social function to which he'd been assigned.

But there had been one encounter when she'd approached him at the governor's inaugural ball and demanded that he get her chauffeur out of the men's room so he could bring her car around.

Logan had gone into the restroom, relayed the message and then come back out.

Madeline Van Waltonscot had been so enraged that he hadn't brought the chauffeur with him that she'd shrieked at him, accused him of being an incompetent fool, called him a pig and generally thrown such a tantrum that a crowd had gathered to see what was wrong.

And when she'd finished with Logan, she'd charged into the men's room and literally dragged out the poor guy who worked for her—red faced and still zipping his pants.

Logan turned off the shower, shaking his head at the memory. "And you're actually considering taking her on as your first client?" he asked himself.

But that was part of his curiosity. He had actively disliked the woman before. Yet the other day he'd had a hard time remembering that.

He'd felt an initial hostility the moment he'd recognized her, but her response to it had been his first surprise. She'd been so polite. And so nervous. So unsure of herself. It was the strangest thing he'd ever seen. It was out of curiosity that he had let her into the house.

But listening to her, watching her, had only confused him all the more.

Maddie.

Had Madeline Van Waltonscot ordered him to call her "your royal highness" he wouldn't have found it odd. But to shorten her name to something warmer and friendlier? And to want the hired help to call her by it? That was amazing.

But there she'd sat, asking him to call her Maddie. And on the edge of her chair, no less. All prim and proper. Dressed in slacks that covered a pair of notoriously gorgeous legs she always used to effect.

Very strange.

And the strangeness had kept up.

She hadn't been furious that he hadn't waited for her to sit before he had. She didn't speak the way he'd recalled.

And she'd answered all his shows of disdain without her trademark animosity and quick temper. She hadn't even taken offense to his laughing at her. Instead she'd sighed forlornly and slumped back in her chair. That was nothing at all like the Madeline Van Waltonscot he'd encountered before. She might have slapped him for his insolence. Or threatened to have him shot.

More incredible still was the fact that she'd actually gone into the kitchen with him. Then she'd shocked the life out of him when she'd rinsed that coffee cup.

Madeline Van Waltonscot rinsing a coffee cup as if it were an everyday occurrence?

He'd have bet she would throw out fine china before lowering herself to do such a thing.

So how would that same person, even if she had adopted her victim's identity in some fluke of mental distress, have thought to do what a lifetime of pampering could not have taught her?

"Knock it off," he ordered himself as he lathered his face to shave. There was no way he would actually consider the body-exchange story as a possibility.

The woman who had come to the office was Madeline Van Waltonscot. In the flesh.

And what well-put-together flesh it was.

She was beautiful, all right, he had to give her that. Exquisite, in fact.

She had silky ebony hair, falling long and straight to just past her shoulders. Peaches-and-cream skin over bones so delicately perfect she looked fragile. A nose that was just a little long—patrician—but thin and too well shaped to be anything but lovely.

She had a lush mouth that was so soft, so supple it didn't seem possible that it usually spewed legendary tirades.

And her eyes...no one else in the world had eyes as bright and unusual a blue as Madeline Van Waltonscot. The dark blue-violet of ripe blueberries...

Logan had lost track of his shaving and suddenly realized it. He frowned into the mirror as he finished and reminded himself that no matter how stunning the woman was, it didn't make any difference. It wasn't as if he were thinking about getting personally involved with her, after all.

He rinsed his razor and threw it into the medicine cabinet, disgusted that he was no closer than he'd been before to making a decision about taking the case.

Or any closer than he'd been before to having any idea what was going on.

The only thing he knew with any certainty was that Madeline Van Waltonscot's new personality was an improvement. A really big improvement. And that if he hadn't been careful, he'd have liked her. Which, coupled with how genuinely beautiful she was, could make for a dangerously potent package in a client who could be in big trouble.

AFTER A MORNING of making more phone calls and a quick lunch back at his apartment, Logan returned to the main house a little before one and found his brother Quinn eating a fast-food hamburger at the kitchen table.

"Finally," Logan greeted the oldest Strummel son. "I've been looking for you for two days. Where the hell have you been?"

"Doing wedding stuff. I think Lindsey and Graham had the right idea in that quick trip to Las Vegas to get married. Clearly our sister knew to avoid the hassle of even a backyard wedding. You wouldn't believe how many things there are to take care of. From dawn until late at night there's something we have to check out or shop for or meet with someone for or somewhere we have to be." Quinn motioned for Logan to sit down. "I'm sorry I haven't been around for your first few days with the agency. Have you been staring at the walls, bored out of your mind?"

"Ha! I've been working."

That surprised his brother, but for a moment he had to chew the bite of burger he'd taken. "You have a client already?"

"I have someone who wants me to take her case," Logan amended. "I've been doing some background checks to decide if I want it. And I've needed to ask you something and been wondering where you and Cara were when you didn't even come home to sleep. I thought Cara was living here now, too."

"She is. But we've spent the last couple of nights at her grandmother's place. It's been so late by the time the three of us finished these wedding deals that we've just slept over."

Logan nodded, having assumed something along those lines. "I called Lindsey about this, but she didn't know anything and I thought maybe you might." At least it was a good bet since the other two Strummel offspring had started the agency long before Logan had joined them.

Quinn gave him a quizzical look while he ate some french fries.

"The woman who wants me to work for her is Madeline Van Waltonscot, the heiress. She showed up here the day before yesterday with a business card for Strummel Investigations. I wondered if you or Lindsey had worked for her before or knew why she had the card. She also told me the most incredible story I've ever heard. And a cop hears a lot of incredible stories."

Quinn's expression turned black and he blew up. "That witch came back here?"

"So she's been here before? I couldn't find a file on her."

"I didn't take the job. About six months ago she wanted to hire me to 'discourage someone' from bothering her. Her lawyer had given her the card, which surprised me because the firm is an old, high-brow one in downtown Denver that we've investigated for before and is hardly apt to encourage thug work. But thug work was sure what it sounded like she wanted. The arrogant, superior, nasty witch."

"So she was herself."

Of course Quinn didn't understand the comment. "Who else would she have been?"

"I'll get to that in a minute. Who did she want you to discourage, and why?"

"I don't know. I didn't let her get far enough to tell me the details. It didn't sound legal or like anything I'd do even if it was. Besides, I didn't like her or her attitude, and all I had to do was hear the 'discourage' part and I politely declined. When my refusal brought out an even uglier side of her, I not so politely asked her to leave. She flung some insults, stormed out and slammed the front door so hard she cracked the jamb. The only thing incredible about that meeting was what an incredible bitch she was. I can't believe she came back."

"Oh, what I'm about to tell you is harder to believe than that." However, the fact that Madeline Van Waltonscot would return after what Quinn described lent some credence to Logan's theory that she was suffering a mental breakdown and had somehow buried memories of herself and her own past. Surely if she had remembered a scene like that one, she'd have chosen another agency to play out a farce. Besides, she hadn't given any sign that she'd been there before or seemed surprised or curious about finding someone other than Quinn to hire. In fact, she'd seemed to have thought Logan was the only investigator there was.

"What did she want this time?" Quinn asked with contempt in his tone.

"Like I said, you're going to find this hard to believe," Logan warned before telling his brother the whole body-exchange story and what Madeline Van Waltonscot now wanted a P.I. for.

When he'd finished, Quinn gave a mirthless snort of a chuckle. "You have to be kidding."

"That's what I said. She just agreed that it was a tough tale to swallow."

"No screaming? No name calling? No disparaging remarks about your family jewels and intelligence?"

"Not a one. She couldn't have been nicer or sweeter."

Quinn shook his head dubiously. "I don't know what her game is, but it would take an act of God to change the shrew I had here six months ago into someone nice or sweet. Still, though, this body-switch story is impossible to believe."

"Except . . ."

"You believe her?"

"No, of course not. But the whole thing just gets more and more strange as I go along. I've had my own dealings with Madeline Van Waltonscot and I didn't like her any better than you do. But even though this is physically the same person, she doesn't seem like the same person." Logan went on to outline the differences. "And when I had people who've known this Maggie Morgan all her life describe what she was like, if I hadn't seen Madeline Van Waltonscot with my own eyes, I would've sworn that the woman sitting across from me the other day and Maggie Morgan were one and the same."

"So you are leaning toward believing her?" Quinn repeated.

"Come on. You think *I'm* out of my mind?" Logan said before explaining the two possibilities he was considering. He still felt obligated to pursue the possibility that something illegal was going on, despite what he did or didn't believe of her body-switch story.

After a moment of thoughtful silence, Quinn said, "Well, brother of mine, I advise you to steer clear of Madeline Van Waltonscot no matter what's going on with her. But you're a full and equal partner in

Strummel Investigations now, which means the cases you accept are up to you. If you do take her on, though, keep a safe distance. Because unless a different entity genuinely has taken over her body, eventually those claws of hers will come out again, and, believe me, she goes for the jugular with them."

"Mmm. That I know."

Quinn cleared his lunch mess, and Logan headed for the office again, intent on making a few more calls before Madeline Van Waltonscot showed up.

When she did, was he going to accept her case or decline it? he asked himself yet again.

This time the question was rhetorical because he knew he couldn't take his brother's advice and steer clear of her. She had him hooked, and he had to know what was really going on with her.

And maybe, at the same time, work out for himself how it was possible that, deep down, he could be the slightest little bit attracted to her.

Of all people.

MADDIE DIDN'T WAIT for the chauffeur to open her door when they reached the office of Strummel Investigations. She let herself out, wished him good luck and sent him on his way. They'd gotten a call on the car phone just a few minutes before, informing him that his wife had been rushed to the hospital in active labor with their first child.

Maddie didn't know what had shocked the poor guy more—the news of his wife, or Maddie telling him he could drop her off and take the car to the hospital. But she was getting used to people being surprised by the "new" Madeline Van Waltonscot.

As Maddie approached the front door, she felt the return of her own nervous excitement at being back there.

She was worried Logan Strummel had decided not to take her case. He might even have called the police to report her as a lunatic on the loose.

She was also nervous because, as much as she didn't want to admit it, she could hardly wait to see the handsome P.I. again.

She'd been trying for two days to keep from thinking about him, picturing him in her mind. She'd been telling herself that an attraction to someone who didn't trust her was even crazier than her current situation.

Nevertheless, his great face kept popping into her thoughts every other minute, causing the same tingling sensation that danced down her spine even now as she climbed the steps to the porch.

It was late, nearly six in the evening, and as she approached the front door she hoped that she hadn't put off coming too long. They hadn't had a fixed appointment, and she'd purposely waited, having yet another chore to do that required the cover of darkness.

Unfortunately, her mission also required a means of transportation and she was fresh out. But if Logan agreed to take her case, maybe she could enlist his help with that matter, too.

In answer to her doorbell ring, Logan's head appeared from inside the office as he spoke on the phone, and he motioned through the screen door for her to come in.

She wasn't sure whether to go into the office while he was still on the phone or wait on the deacon's bench in the hallway, so she approached the office hesitantly, peeking in to see if maybe he might be wrapping up the call.

One glance inside told her to stay in the hall. Not only was Logan still on the telephone, but he wasn't alone. Another man was hunkered down in front of the detective's desk, gathering papers that had apparently fallen to the floor.

She'd have just backed up except that the other man, who was in profile to her, seemed to catch sight of her out of the corner of his eye.

"Don't mind me. I didn't know Logan had a client with him. I'll just wait out here until he's ready for me," she assured the man in a whisper.

"That's all right. I'm not a client," he said amicably as he slipped the last paper into a file and stood. But one glance at her hardened the features on a face that resembled Logan's.

"I should probably sit out here until he's finished with his call, anyway," she added, taking refuge on the deacon's bench after all.

The other man followed her as far as the doorway, leaning a shoulder there, crossing his arms over a chest not as broad as Logan's and pinning her in place with eyes that were a similar but paler color. "Madeline Van Waltonscot," he said.

It was always hard to know if people who recognized her had known the heiress or merely seen her picture in the society pages. Since there was no way of knowing, she did what had now become habit.

"Maddie, please," she said, wanting to add "and you are..."

But too often in the past three weeks when she took that tack she'd found herself in odd positions with people the heiress was well acquainted with.

This particular man seemed intent on unnerving her with his gaze, and all she could do was give him a small smile and hope he'd say something that would clue her in to how well he knew the heiress.

"Quinn. Quinn Strummel," he finally offered.

"You must be Logan's brother. The one who lives in this neat old house," she answered, hoping to distract him by getting onto a new subject.

"You like the house?" he asked skeptically.

"Very much. These older homes have so much more warmth and character than newer ones. And they're a lot more fun to decorate. They usually have such interesting nooks and crannies that have so many possibilities." She was babbling, which always happened when she was nervous.

"You're an expert on decorating, are you?"

He shot the questions as if they were part of an inquisition, and Maddie wondered how much Logan had told him. But she didn't know what to do except answer. "I wouldn't say I was an expert, no. It's just what I—" she'd almost said "what I do" but realized she didn't *do* anything these days "—what I'm interested in," she amended.

"Are you?" he said in a challenging tone.

The man was trying to provoke her, and Maddie couldn't take the tension that was mounting in her by the moment. She decided to cut to the chase. Very politely she said, "Mr. Strummel, did Logan tell you about my situation and what's going on with me?"

"Quinn," he said, rather than answering her query. "Feel free to call me Quinn. Or bonehead if you prefer. I believe that was one of the many and varied names you called me when we last met."

She flinched. These situations were the worst— when the heiress had alienated a person with her sharp tongue in the past.

She could hardly go into the whole explanation to get herself off the hook, and often the hostility was hard to surmount. The best she could do was try an all-purpose apology and once more attempt to skirt the issue.

"I'm sorry for whatever might have happened before. I—"

Logan appeared in the doorway behind his brother just then and saved her from floundering for another change of subject.

"You giving her a hard time?" he asked the man named Quinn.

"It's okay," she answered before he could. "He probably has cause."

Still, Quinn Strummel gored her with his gaze. "You know, Miss Van Waltonscot—"

"Maddie, please."

"I swore that if I ever had to be in the same room with you again I was going to give you a piece of my mind."

She nodded, squared her shoulders as if to face a firing squad and said politely, "If it'll make you feel better, go ahead. Then maybe when the air is clear we can start over," she finished on a hopeful note.

Something about her words made him laugh, but it wasn't a pleasant sound. "And you'll just sit there and take it?" he asked incredulously.

"Okay, that's enough," Logan said, sounding very much like a cop breaking up an unpleasant scene.

After another moment of staring at her, Logan's brother glanced over his shoulder. "You're right, she's pretty convincing." He pushed off the jamb, shaking his head as he did, and stepped out of the doorway. "At any rate, I don't have time for any more of this. I'll leave you kids to do whatever it is you're going to do." But to Logan he added, "Just remember what I told you."

Logan nodded and watched his brother go into the kitchen, where the sound of Quinn leaving through the back door came almost immediately.

Then Logan looked back at Maddie, who felt immeasurably better to be alone with him once again. In fact, better than she wished she felt.

"I expected you earlier this afternoon," he said.

"I have something else I need to do out this way after we talk. In fact, I could actually use your help in doing it if you take my case. But anyway, that's why I came late. I hope it's okay."

She saw a flash of suspicion jump across his features, but it was fleeting and he didn't comment. Instead he tossed a nod over his shoulder at the office beyond and said, "Come on in and let's talk."

She followed him, noticing that when she got there he was standing, this time waiting for her to sit before taking his own seat behind the desk.

Did better manners and stepping in to protect her from his brother mean he was going to work for her?

"I've spoken to a lot of people who knew Maggie Morgan," he began.

"Designs Unlimited?"

"No, not Designs Unlimited. I've left three messages with their secretary, but they haven't returned my calls yet. The people I spoke to are in Kansas. People who knew Maggie Morgan growing up.''

He seemed to wait for a reaction from her. She didn't know how he expected her to respond so she merely nodded.

"Maggie Morgan was born—"

"June 11, 1959," she finished before he could, anxious to prove herself.

He raised an eyebrow at her. "Her parents were both born in—"

"Nineteen twenty-nine, two days apart—September 19 and 21."

"In Kansas City, Kansas. And the Morgan family lived at—"

"Sixty-seven ninety-one Somerset Drive."

"And Curtis Morgan was head minister of—"

"The First United Methodist Church of Fieldstone, Kansas."

He paused. "All a matter of public record." Obviously her showing off knowledge of her life history wasn't convincing him of anything.

Then he went on. "Maggie Morgan attended—"

"Fieldstone West High School and graduated in 1976. A year early because I skipped third grade." She could see that she'd surprised him a little, but he hid it quickly.

"The principal there now—"

"Is Doris Padilla. She taught math when I was there but was promoted to assistant principal the year after I graduated and then to full principal three years later."

"And although Maggie Morgan was nominated for secretary of her junior class, she declined to run."

"Not a matter of public record, but I wanted to be class president, instead. And—I'm not proud of this— if I couldn't be president I didn't want to be anything at all."

He smiled and she knew she'd surprised him again. "That was Mrs. Padilla's guess as to why you—why Maggie Morgan declined the nomination." He cocked that handsome head of his to one side. "And Maggie Morgan was almost not allowed to go through the graduation ceremony because she insisted on wearing red shoes."

"That's not true. I don't know who told you that, but it's a lie. I'd have never done anything that wild, let alone go up against school authorities. Who said that?"

He just stared at her for a long moment until light dawned in her. "Oh, I get it. You made it up. You were trying to trick me. To see if I'd confirm something that hadn't happened so I'd sound like an expert when I'm really not."

He went on studying her a little longer and then said, "Madeline Van Waltonscot was born June 11, 1959."

This time he'd surprised her. "She was? We were born on the same day?"

He'd been leaning forward and now sat back in his chair and looked at her over his steepled fingers the way he had the last time they'd faced each other across the desk.

But he didn't answer her question, and she really wanted to know so she asked again. "Is that true? Did we honestly have the same birth date or are you just trying to trick me again?"

"It's true that Madeline Van Waltonscot and Maggie Morgan were both born on June 11, 1959."

Maddie hadn't realized she was sitting slightly forward, too, until she sank back herself. "Wow. So much for astrology because we sure weren't anything alike. So you suppose that's how this cosmic joke got going? That maybe fate put us in the wrong place all those years ago and just corrected the mistake now?"

He laughed a little, shaking his head and still staring at her over those hands that she couldn't help noticing were the most masculine, sexy-looking things she'd ever laid eyes on. "Cosmic joke?" he repeated.

She shrugged. "I don't know what else to call it. Do you?"

Time to change the subject again, she thought, when he didn't respond. "So," she said. "Have I passed the test? Will you take my case?"

She wondered if staring was in the Strummel genes because that's what he went on doing for the longest time.

He finally said, "Yes, I'll take the case. But understand that I'll be watching you, and if I find a hole in this story of yours or come across any wrongdoing—"

"I know. You'll blow me out of the water."

"In the blink of an eye."

Now that they were through setting the ground rules, she got down to business—and distracted herself from that smoldering gaze of his.

Maddie opened her purse and took out the audio tape she'd retrieved from her answering machine. "There was another call this morning while I was out taking a walk. I thought—if you accepted the case— you might want to hear it for yourself."

He took the tape, popped the top on his own machine on the desk and replaced his with hers. When he pushed the play button, a very aggravated male voice said, "You're pushing this too far, Madeline. How can you live with yourself? How can you get up in the morning and face yourself in the mirror? I'm warning you—light any more fires and you may find me burning you back."

"That's it," Maddie said as the sound of a phone being slammed down came onto the tape before it went silent.

Logan rewound it and listened again. "I want to keep this," he told her, holding up the tape she'd brought.

"Okay."

"You still don't recognize the voice?"

"No. I only know it doesn't belong to Bent Nose."

"Any word from him?"

"No. Nothing."

Logan stood and went to a cabinet behind his desk, leaning over slightly to take a manila envelope from a bottom drawer. He turned back to the desk to mark the tape and put it in the envelope, which he then placed in a file she noticed was entitled Madeline Van Waltonscot.

So he'd decided to take the case even before she arrived; Maddie didn't know whether that was a good sign or a bad one.

Then he propped a hip on the corner of his desk, and she had to drag her gaze upward from there.

"What is it you wanted my help with tonight?"

She stole a glance out the window, seeing that the sun was nearly down.

"Before the accident I was renting a house in Wheat Ridge. Only about fifteen minutes from here."

"You—Madeline Van Waltonscot?"

"Me—Maggie Morgan. I went by there today and spied in the windows to see if my belongings were still there. Of course they aren't, but luckily the house is vacant. I need to get in because I had some things hidden—valuables—that I'm reasonably sure the owner wouldn't have come across when he cleared the place out."

"You have a key?"

"Well, I did have, of course. But at the moment I don't have anything of my own—"

"Meaning Maggie Morgan?"

She nodded. "So I don't have the key, either. I'm sure it was returned to the owner."

"Then how do you plan to get in?"

"The lock on one of the bedroom windows doesn't work. I can get in through there. I did it a bunch of times when I forgot my purse, but I didn't want to do it in broad daylight today."

"You're talking about breaking and entering."

"Not to vandalize or steal or do something bad. I just want back what's rightfully mine."

"It's still breaking and entering."

"Only technically. I have a lease on the house until January and a damage deposit and the last month's rent paid in advance. That's all money I'll never get back. The least it should give me is the right to go in just this once and get what was left behind. But how can I show up with this face and ask the owner to let me in? I can't even go and make up a story about who I am because Madeline Van Waltonscot is too well known. The most I could do was call the owner today and say I was a friend—''

"Of Maggie Morgan's?"

"Right. And ask what happened to my furniture and clothes and things. He said that since there was no next of kin he'd given the bulk of it to charity, but sent some of my personal belongings to Designs Unlimited in case someone there might want a remembrance of me. He didn't know what they'd done with them, and I'm hoping when you talk to them, you'll ask," she ended with that hopeful note in her voice again.

"Take a breath and get back to the original subject," he advised patiently.

She forced herself to slow down. "Here's what I'd planned. I was going to have the chauffeur drive me to the rental house after you and I had finished here. I hate being driven around in that showy car but I guess the one Madeline Van Waltonscot wrecked was the only one she owned besides the limousine, and I can't drive the limousine because it's too big. Anyway, the chauffeur's wife is having their baby and he had to drop me off, so I was wondering if maybe I could persuade you to—''

Logan put his hand up to stop the runaway train of words. "How about if I call the owner tomorrow, say I'm the husband of the friend whom he spoke to today, trump up an excuse and see if I can't get him to let me in?"

She shook her head. "I have to do it. The hiding place is complicated to find and get into."

Logan frowned at her, creasing lines between his brows and sobering her enthusiasm considerably. "I will not aid and abet you in committing a crime."

"But how is it a crime when I have a legal right to the place and to what was left there?"

"Maggie Morgan has a legal right to the place and what was left there."

"I know things only Maggie Morgan could know," she said, reminding him of their earlier game. "And if I show you a secret hiding place only I—she—" Maddie rolled her eyes. "It would be so much easier if you'd just concede who I am for conversational purposes. If I can show you a secret hiding place that only Maggie Morgan knew about, wouldn't that help things between us and make you feel better about taking my case, too?"

She watched Logan's handsome features as he considered her argument.

And since his even considering it felt like an advantage, she pressed it. "Come on. It'll help you and me both and it won't do any harm. No one else is living there yet."

For a long moment he stared at her again, clearly debating with himself.

But she had really surprised him before, and she thought his curiosity was piqued, too. She offered just one "Please," and that was it.

"If this isn't on the level I'm dropping this case altogether."

"Agreed." She could have hugged him, she was so glad he was going to help. And once that thought flashed through her mind, it was much, much too titillating, and she could feel her face begin to heat with a blush.

She stood quickly and spun toward the door. "Let's get to it, then," she suggested too brightly.

But he didn't follow her. Instead, from his perch on the desk, he said, "Your clothes are too light for cat burglary."

She hadn't thought of that and turned back to him, grimacing down at the yellow pantsuit she wore. "You don't know what I wouldn't give for a pair of blue jeans."

"Why haven't you gone out and bought some?"

She made a face. "I just don't feel right spending money that doesn't seem like my own. I mean, I guess that's crazy and of course I'll have to, but it's very weird. And to tell you the truth, I don't know exactly how I'm going to do it, anyway. There's very little cash that I've come across, and I'm afraid to write checks or sign credit card receipts because my signature isn't the same."

He shook his head as if he regretted asking the question in the first place.

She wanted to say "think how I feel," but then it occurred to her he might start to wonder how he was going to get paid. "Don't worry about your fee, though. Bills like that go to the accountant—except I think he's called something more impressive than that, business manager or something. Anyhow, bills are taken care of that way. It's just the everyday stuff I'm sort of stuck on."

"Come on. I think there's a pair of my sister's jeans around here—if they were put back by the last damsel in distress they were loaned to. You can wear them and a shirt of mine for your first caper."

A HALF HOUR LATER, dressed in jeans that were on the baggy side and a much too big navy blue shirt of Logan's, Maddie directed him to the rental house in the early-evening darkness.

The house was a tiny ranch-style box that sat far back from the road amid several giant evergreen trees that virtually obscured it.

Logan pulled onto the dirt drive and went all the way up to the side of the house, leaving his Jeep barely visible from the street.

"If you have to be a cat burglar, isn't this the perfect place?" Maddie asked, as if they were embarking on a great adventure.

Logan merely glanced at her from the corner of his eye and turned off the engine.

"The bedroom window is around back," she informed him as they got out.

The trees blocked any light from the moon or from the streetlights, leaving deep shadows that blinded them. Luckily Maddie knew the way and warned Logan when to step up onto the bricked walkway that led to the rear of the property, also pointing out a geranium pot just around the corner of the porch where a cat was curled up asleep.

"Hi, Priscilla," Maddie greeted the animal, stopping to scratch it behind the ear as she explained, "She belongs to the people next door." Then she apologized to the tabby for not having more time to pet it, pointed to the three panels of glass that made up the bedroom window and headed for it. "That's the one with the broken lock," she said.

She maneuvered the screen on the center pane until she'd worked it free and set it aside. Then she gave the glass a nudge and it swung inward.

"Nothing like a secure house," Logan murmured from nearby.

"I used to have a bench out here that I'd climb on, but now that everything is gone, could you give me a boost?"

"Anything that'll get this over with." He kneeled on the ground, one knee to the earth, one up, and patted his thigh invitingly. "Step up."

Her pulse did a little dance at the thought of touching him, but what else could she do?

She kicked off her low-heeled pumps and put a hand on one of his shoulders.

She hated that she was so aware of his nearness but she couldn't help it. It was as if she were a battery and he the charger. Her nerve endings seemed to wake up and take notice of even the way it felt to have the sole of her foot against the hardness of his thigh.

Banishing her traitorous thoughts, Maddie used the sill to pull herself up and hiked her other leg through the window, pushing it open farther as she did so. Straddling the sill, she began to ease her other leg into the window opening.

That was when she got stuck.

She'd done this a half dozen times before. But always in a different body. And at a scant five feet tall and ninety-five pounds, she had fit better than this new five-foot-three, 107-pound model did.

Both of her arms were through and braced on either side of her on the inside sill, but there really wasn't anything to grab on to for leverage.

One leg dangled uselessly inside and the other was jammed between her body and the frame.

She wiggled. She scooted. She lunged.

She just didn't budge.

"Maddie?" Logan said from behind her in that deep, smoked-wood voice of his.

"We have a small problem."

"You're stuck."

"Maybe you could give me a little shove."

"Through the window and onto the floor? I'd hurt you."

She wiggled again. To no avail. "I don't think there's another choice."

"Let me try," he suggested with a weary sigh.

There she was, trapped in an awkward position in a window and still alarmingly aware of his hands pushing carefully against her back, against her thigh, against her rear end, in an attempt to ease her through.

"It's not working," she finally told him. At least it wasn't working on her predicament in the window. It was definitely working at sending more of those sparks to glitter all along the surface of her skin. "I'm sorry," she added over her shoulder. "If you want to leave and call the cops or the fire department from a safe distance away so you aren't here when they come to pry me out, I'll understand."

She heard him laugh, for the first time sounding genuinely amused, and it warmed and delighted her much more than it should have. Especially under the circumstances.

"I'm not going to leave you," he assured. "What kind of lock is on the back door?"

"Just a pretty old one in the door handle. There's no dead bolt or anything, if that's what you mean."

"That's what I mean. Let me see if I can work it open and get you out from the inside."

"You pick locks?"

"I can't answer that on the grounds that it might incriminate me," he recited.

"Why didn't you just get us in that way in the first place?" she asked.

"This is your caper, remember?" he answered. Then he said, "Just sit tight."

"As if I could do anything else."

Thank God he was being a good sport about this.

Apparently he was a talented lock picker. She heard the door open a few minutes later, and he said, "I'm in. I'll be right there."

And he was, too, turning on the overhead light as he came into the room, shaking his head at her. "You're a lot of trouble, lady," he announced in a teasing tone.

"It's the body. It's different than when I did this before."

He laughed at that, too.

"No, really it is. This body was my first big surprise when I woke up from that coma."

"I imagine it would be. Let's just see how we're going to get you out of there so I can turn off this light before somebody spots us in here."

His touch was no less powerful than before, and Maddie had to fight the sensations as he worked her leg carefully through the window frame until it was free. Then he clamped both hands on either side of her waist and lifted her down.

By virtue of necessity she landed close in front of him, but that closeness took her by surprise, anyway.

Or maybe it was the current that suddenly seemed to pass between them.

She wasn't the only one feeling it, because when she looked up at Logan she found his expression sober again, those vertical lines back between his brows. And his full lips parted just slightly, as if he were about to kiss someone.

Her.

Only she realized that he wasn't moving to do any such thing. She was just wishing he would.

She took a quick step backward; so did he, even as the air around them still seemed to sizzle.

"I don't want to be here any longer than we have to," he said gruffly. Or was there something other than gruffness and impatience that had put that husky tone in his voice?

"We need to go into the bathroom," she answered, wishing her own voice didn't have such a breathy quality to it.

But still he stood there in front of her, separated by only a few feet, staring down at her with those heather gray eyes for a long moment before he went to the switch and turned off the light. "Come on, then, lead the way."

Maddie swallowed with some difficulty and forced herself to move, wishing that just passing in front of him out the bedroom door didn't reignite the sparks all over again.

The bathroom was fairly large but didn't have a window, so it seemed safe to turn on the light. Maddie went to the shower stall that was beside a claw-footed bathtub, instantly aware of Logan following her into the small space.

She pointed to the top of one of the three tiled walls. "It's up there. Not quite in the middle of the first and second rows. The tiles fell on my head one morning, and behind them is a vent. I don't know why anybody put a vent in the shower or why someone would think they could just tile over the grate and have the tile stay, but that's the way it is. I thought it was a terrific hiding place so I duct-taped the tile to the grate. First you have to unstick the tile, then the grate has to be jiggled to get it loose. My things are in the vent.''

She stepped to one side of the stall so Logan could get in and redirected him when he misjudged which tiles were the loose ones. Then she coached his technique until he finally worked the grate free.

''You'll have to reach into the vent.''

He did and came out with a small wooden box.

She heard him mutter ''amazing'' to himself, but she was more interested in what he'd retrieved for her.

Once he'd handed it over she didn't even move to let him out of the stall before opening the lid to make sure the contents were still there.

''Oh, you don't know how glad I am to have these back,'' she breathed, taking the contents out one item at a time to let him see what they were. ''This is my mother's engagement ring and these are both my parents' wedding rings,'' she said, setting them in Logan's palm. ''This is the Golden Gloves charm my father won as a boxer when he was a young man. And this is the silver locket my mother wore around her neck every day from when my father gave it to her when I was born until she died. It has my father's picture on one side and my baby picture on the other. See?''

She opened the charm so he could look at the photographs. Then she closed her fist around the locket as if it were a talisman that would give her good luck, holding it that way for a moment before replacing it. ''That's all there is,'' she told him with a sigh. ''There are some mementos and pictures and things I hope maybe someone at Designs Unlimited kept, but it really would have crushed me to have lost these.''

She realized suddenly that Logan was being very quiet and glanced up at him. He held the jewelry box in his hand but was looking at her very solemnly, very intently, very curiously.

"You just can't believe that inside I'm really Maggie Morgan, can you?" she guessed.

He didn't answer. He just went on watching her, though this time his staring didn't unnerve her. This time it wasn't actually staring. He was delving into her eyes with his, holding her with them.

And for the second time kissing crossed her mind with a potent wish that he'd do so.

He broke the spell, handing back the jewelry. "We should get out of here. I'll go outside and hand you the bedroom screen to put back. Then lock up and come out."

Maddie nodded her agreement and went into the other room to wait for him.

Whatever had passed between them was forgotten.

Maddie insisted that he take her back to his office, where she called a cab to take her home so she wouldn't put him to any more bother.

And also so she wouldn't be alone in the car with him any longer than she absolutely needed to be.

"What's on the agenda for tomorrow?" she asked while they stood together in the doorway of Quinn's house waiting for the taxi.

"I'm going to get persistent with Designs Unlimited until I reach someone who'll agree to see me. I want to talk about Maggie Morgan and about anything they might have overheard or seen going on with Madeline Van Waltonscot."

"Maybe if they have any of my stuff left you could get them to give it to you?"

"I'll see what I can do. But you don't sound too enthusiastic about it. Why is that?"

"I was hoping to enlist your help again."

"More cat burglary?"

"No. A board meeting. I tried to make excuses to the man who called me about it, but he was just going to postpone again, so I finally agreed to it. It's tomorrow afternoon. And I'm scared witless to go alone. I don't know anything about board meetings."

"I was a cop, remember?" he said. "I've never been to a board meeting, either."

"I was just hoping for a little moral support," she hedged. How could she tell him that since waking from the coma he was the only person she'd encountered whom she felt comfortable with? More than comfortable with. When she was with him she felt safe. Secure. Bolstered and better able to play out her charade.

"I don't suppose it would be a bad idea for me to be there. It's possible Bent Nose and the business are connected in some way, and maybe we'll come across a clue as to how or why."

Her spirits rose. "Then you'll come?" she asked, hating that she sounded like a schoolgirl who'd just invited a boy she had a crush on to a dance and he'd accepted.

"Yes, I'll come."

"It's at two."

The cab pulled up in front of Quinn's house just then and honked. Before Maddie thought better of it, she stood on tiptoe and kissed Logan's cheek. "Thank you," she heard herself murmur.

It really was a reflex of gratitude that had spurred her, but once she'd done it, that earlier electrical current was lit again, leaving her uneasy and flustered.

"Tomorrow, then," she said in a hurry, rushing out the screen door before he had a chance to say or do anything.

But from the taxi's window she saw Logan standing on his brother's porch, watching her intently. All she could think was that she couldn't wait until they were together again.

But it didn't have anything to do with the case.

Or with gratitude.

Chapter Three

The Van Waltonscot home was a three-story Southern-plantation-style house on two acres of ultraprime real estate in Denver's upscale Cherry Creek section, just a stone's throw from the elite Denver Country Club, and much, much farther from anything Maddie was accustomed to.

On the ground floor was a four-star-restaurant-size kitchen as scrubbed and bright as a hospital operating room; a dining room with a marble table that would seat seventy-two; a living room large enough to need six full sofas, a dozen chairs scattered about and more tables, lamps and knickknacks than she'd had a chance to look at in any detail.

There was also a theater, a ballroom, a den, an office for the house manager and Bernice the personal assistant, several elaborate bathrooms, a wing in which the live-in servants had quarters and an entranceway big enough to land small aircraft.

From the grand foyer rose a curved staircase that swept like a woman's twirled skirt up and around an opera-house-size chandelier that dropped from the glass-domed ceiling of the highest level, down through the ornately carved railings that marked the second and third floors.

The middle level held ten guest rooms and baths—color-coded marvels complete with private saunas, fireplaces, televisions, stereo systems and well-stocked wet bars, as well as antique feather beds, armoires and bureaus.

The upper level had only three suites, and since Maddie occupied one of them she assumed that had been the family's floor—when there had been a family in residence, as surely there must have been at some point with a house this huge. She didn't know anything about the heiress's background and didn't find the stoic old portraits that lined the wall alongside the stairs particularly informative. In fact, the whole house had more an air of museum than real home.

Each suite included a bedroom and bathroom fit for a whole harem, attached to an equally large office and sitting room. Together they made up living space with more square footage than the entire rental house Maddie and Logan had broken into the night before.

If there had been a kitchen in her suite she could have easily survived without ever using any of the remainder of the house. And she would have preferred it.

What she'd discovered in the past three weeks was that being a spoiled heiress was not easy. At least not for someone who had lived alone and independently for a number of years now.

In fact she'd taken to tiptoeing around, carrying her shoes rather than wearing them across those polished floors, particularly the hand-painted Italian tile of the rotundalike entryway.

And there were servants on duty even in the wee hours of the morning, anticipating her every movement and desire.

Who would have thought being waited on hand and foot would be a pain in the neck?

When there was a knock at the bedroom door at precisely 11:45, Maddie opened it knowing exactly who would be out in the hallway even before she set eyes on the woman.

Bernice, the personal assistant.

An impeccably clad elderly lady with graying black hair and sharp cheekbones. Her spine was always ramrod straight, shoulders back, in a militarylike stance. She spoke in a monotone and she did not smile.

Maddie invited her in and Bernice took only three steps across the threshold before stopping. She stood as still as a statue, hands clasped in front of her, waiting expectantly.

It seemed strange that there wasn't any sort of warmth or friendship or bond between the personal assistant and the heiress, but Maddie had learned that unless she opened the conversation, Bernice would merely stand there at the ready, not speaking until she was spoken to.

As usual Maddie tried a simple, friendly, "How are you today?"

The woman answered like a robot. "Fine, thank you, Miss Van Waltonscot." And offered nothing more.

By now Maddie knew what the personal assistant was there to do. She was waiting to be instructed on Maddie's choice of clothing for the day, which she would then retrieve from the vast closet and set out.

Maddie hated the whole process, made worse by the fact that she had no true familiarity with the wardrobe and couldn't perform her part believably.

So far she'd been forced to pretend she didn't have any preference and leave the selections to the personal assistant. The consequence was feeling like a child again, dressed every day in what someone else picked out for her.

And although it had been bad enough to convalesce in silk peignoirs and negligees when she'd been longing for the oversize T-shirt she ordinarily wore to bed, or a good old sweat suit, she hadn't at all liked meeting with Logan in clothes chosen for her by someone else.

"I've been thinking, and from now on I'm going to go ahead and get my own clothes out in the mornings. If that's okay."

A flash of what almost looked like fear crossed the assistant's face—the first hint of emotion Bernice had ever shown. "I'm sorry if I've—"

"Nothing's wrong," Maddie assured her quickly. "I just want to do it for myself."

Bernice looked uneasy. "I can't tell you how sorry I am—"

"Really. This isn't a criticism. I just want to handle it myself from here on."

Bernice watched her in a way Maddie was getting used to. Wary. Confused. As if she were silently preparing herself for the boom to be lowered. So this time Maddie tried for some confidential girl talk to reassure the other woman.

"It's really silly, when you think about it. I'm a grown woman, I can certainly get my own clothes out of the closet. Surely you have enough to do."

"I don't mind. Honestly."

"I'm glad to hear it. Still, I'm just going to take over this one chore."

Confidential girl talk didn't help, either. The other woman went on staring at her, her face white with what looked like panic. "Please, Miss Van Waltonscot. I need this job. I'm raising my grandson and he's about to go to college and—"

"It's okay," Maddie told her in a hurry, hating that anything she'd said had prompted that pleading note in the elderly woman's voice. "Please don't take offense and don't worry that I'm going to fire you, because I'm not." In fact, had Maddie felt more free with the heiress's money, she'd have given the personal assistant a raise to help with that college tuition and to convince Bernice that she wasn't unhappy with her.

"You can still oversee everything getting laundered and ironed and kept up. I appreciate that. You really are doing a terrific job. Just consider yourself let off the hook for this one thing."

Bernice nodded and turned to go out.

"Have a nice day," Maddie called after her.

The poor woman seemed unsure of what repercussions might yet befall her, but there was nothing Maddie could do about it. Time, she hoped, would convince everyone that they were not going to have their heads bitten off each time she opened her mouth.

Meanwhile, it felt good to finally be free to choose what she was going to wear herself, so she wasted no time in heading for the closet.

Cavernous. That was the only word for the windowless space the size of a one-bedroom apartment. It was lucky everything in it was well organized.

Evening gowns and fur storage were farthest back, kept separate by mechanical floor-to-ceiling cedar shoe compartments that rotated at the flick of a switch.

Dresses, skirts and suits took up the middle two-thirds of the closet, with slacks, blazers, blouses and sweaters accounting for the front portion, which also had several shelves and dresser drawers built right into the walls.

Maddie searched through the business suits that any working woman would have died to own. Not only were they beautifully tailored in a fabric for every season, but there were so many of them that months could pass without wearing the same thing twice.

She opted for a silver-gray suit that reminded her of Logan's eyes—not that that had anything to do with anything, she assured herself. The color was just more sedate than the bright pink and yellow of what she'd worn before, more befitting a board meeting, Maddie thought.

It was subtly sophisticated, with a long jacket that buttoned diagonally from the right hip upward to the left shoulder, worn over a short, tight skirt.

She also had no complaint with the underwear available to her. Silk panties and lacy bras the quality of which she'd never seen in any department store. At least not in any of the department stores she could afford to frequent. The garments were so exquisitely sheer, soft and sexy that each time in the last three weeks that she'd put on one of the matching sets, she'd felt deliciously, secretly sensual.

"If only you knew, Logan Strummel."

But that stopped her just as she was about to reach for a pair of flame red bikinis and a plunging bra to go with them.

She'd been thinking about the investigator nearly every waking hour since meeting him. She just couldn't seem to help it. But having him in mind when she chose her underwear?

"Logan Strummel and underwear cannot be in the same thought," she stressed to herself. That really was going too far. Just the way kissing him the night before—even on the cheek—had been.

And yet that flash of memory sent a little tingle all through her.

She could still feel his skin, warm and masculine, against her mouth as vividly as if it had been much more than a split second's worth of contact.

This was no time to be attracted to anyone, she reminded herself. Even if he was terrific looking and intelligent and sexier than he had any business being.

Not only was the timing lousy, she knew he didn't trust her as far as he could see her. So being attracted to him was doubly out of the question.

Besides, she might not have any control over who she was now or what the old Madeline Van Waltonscot had done in the past, but she was determined to get a firm grip on the present and future. To that end, she could certainly control her own feelings; in a life gone haywire, she needed to.

So what if thoughts of Logan kept her up at night? If her mind's eye kept remembering every detail of that chiseled face? So what if she couldn't keep from wondering what made him tick, from wondering if he was involved with anyone? So what if she spent every minute away from him wanting to be with him again, wanting to get to know him?

Okay, sometimes the attraction to him did feel pretty powerful and she seemed too weak to resist it.

Like the night before when she'd thought...
hoped... that he might kiss her at the rental house.

There were enough things she had to figure out, to
come to grips with. Her own feelings about what had
happened to her since the accident were so unsettled,
she was so unsettled. The last thing she needed—or
wanted—was to add the complication of romance.

Not that he seemed to be offering it...

She took her hands away from the red underwear
and picked up a pale tan pair that, while no less elegant, were more demure just by virtue of the color.
Then she closed the drawer of the built-in dresser and
went to decide on shoes.

The bottom line, she told herself, was that she could
feel relieved at finally having told someone her secret.
She could be grateful to have help sorting through
everything. She could even enjoy being herself around
at least one person.

But that was as far as it could go.

"I mean it," she told herself for emphasis.

Except that once she'd chosen a pair of low-heeled
pumps, gathered everything up and headed out of the
closet, her bare feet veered to that lingerie drawer
again.

And she traded the tan underwear for the red, after
all.

LOGAN WASN'T GOOD at waiting. Which was just what
he was doing, sitting in his car across the street from
the office of Designs Unlimited at 12:45 that afternoon. The place was closed for lunch, but he had an
appointment with the owner, who had assured him
she'd be back by 12:30.

She hadn't made it.

And waiting for her left him thinking about one of the differences between being a cop and a P.I.

If he were still a cop, he'd have shown up that morning without calling for an appointment.

Even if he'd called ahead as a cop, odds were he wouldn't have been kept waiting. More than likely Janine Taylor would have made sure to be there when he'd arrived.

But then in a lot of respects it was tougher to be a P.I. The jobs were similar, but a private investigator didn't have the authority of the badge. And he suffered a twinge of regret at the fact that the badge wasn't his to carry anymore.

Not that leaving the force hadn't been his idea. But some decisions didn't get made happily.

He'd wanted to be a cop from the time he was a little kid, like his father and his grandfather before that. Like Quinn planned to be, too.

But joining the force hadn't merely been a family tradition. Logan had loved the idea of helping people in trouble, of keeping peace and order. He'd never envisioned himself doing anything else. Even when things had turned sour, he'd tried to keep at it, to make it right again.

It just hadn't worked out. Not for him. Not for Quinn, either, who'd left the force because he'd gotten fed up with the bureaucracy and started Strummel Investigations with their sister Lindsey.

Quinn's leaving had been easier, Logan knew, because it wasn't the result of wrestling with a moral dilemma.

"Water under the bridge," he muttered to himself.

Besides, on the up side, if Maddie had come to the station with this case when he was still a cop, he'd have had to refer her to a psychiatrist. Then word would have gotten out about her body-exchange tale and everyone would have cracked wise. Maybe even him.

But now the thought of the way it might have played out, of Maddie being a laughingstock, raised his ire.

Strange that he felt so protective of her, he thought. And the strength of that protectiveness made him wonder something else. It made him wonder if he was beginning to actually believe her.

Maybe. Because he sure couldn't jump right in and say he didn't, the way he had before.

Not that he was buying into the whole thing. But the more time he spent with Maddie, the more he began to consider that his eyes might be deceiving him—that there was an outside chance he shouldn't believe so much in what he saw and should instead start paying attention to what he sensed in her.

Because what he sensed was that she really wasn't Madeline Van Waltonscot anymore. For whatever reason. And that the change ran deep.

Or maybe he was just trying to convince himself that the present Madeline Van Waltonscot wasn't the same as the past one because it made his own attraction to the heiress more palatable.

That was a sobering thought. Yet he couldn't deny he was attracted to her. Big time.

"Hell," he murmured in self-disgust.

What could he have been thinking when he nearly kissed her last night at that rental house?

He hadn't been thinking at all, that was the problem. He'd just been following the sense that she wasn't the heiress. That she really was a down-to-earth, funny, spunky, humble, Kansas-born minister's daughter who had somehow slipped under his skin when he wasn't looking.

He liked her. He enjoyed her company.

And yes, he'd definitely wanted to kiss her.

When she'd pecked that parting kiss on his cheek, what little restraint he'd been hanging on to up until then had flown out the window and he'd nearly grabbed her for a second, more serious round.

But he hadn't and he wasn't going to.

He also wasn't kidding himself; the attraction to her was strong. And resisting it wasn't going to be any easier than figuring out just what, exactly, was going on inside that pretty head of hers.

He couldn't let himself be drawn into feelings that might cloud the issues. Feelings that might blind him. Yet he also had a gut instinct that he didn't need to worry about being on guard, not with Maddie at least.

"Maybe you're just being royally, elaborately suckered," he argued with himself.

Even so, he recalled what he'd seen with his own eyes when she'd taken the things out of the little jewelry box. Inexpensive pieces that didn't have any more than sentimental value. But they'd meant something to her.

And in that moment of watching Maddie's reaction to the trinkets, he hadn't doubted that those two women were not one and the same.

Only how could that be? It was a question he'd been asking himself since then.

He didn't have an answer. He just plain didn't know. He just plain didn't know anything.

So where did that leave him?

Confused. And getting more confused by the minute.

Except about one thing—she was off-limits. And somehow he was not, absolutely not, going to give in to his attraction to her.

Just then a woman of about fifty finally pulled into the parking lot for Designs Unlimited, got out of her car and went to the glass front door to unlock it.

Grateful to be distracted from his thoughts and frustrating feelings for Maddie, Logan didn't waste any time leaving his Jeep and following the woman inside.

"Janine Taylor?" he asked when she glanced up from putting her purse in a desk drawer.

"You must be Mr. Strummel," she responded with a small, grim smile. "I'm sorry for being late. Lunch with a client can sometimes be hard to get away from."

Logan nodded but didn't comment. Instead he got down to business. "As I told you on the phone, Miss Van Waltonscot hired me to find any next of kin for Maggie Morgan and return whatever might be left of her things."

"I suppose that's Miss Van Waltonscot's idea of making amends," the designer said more to herself than to him.

He ignored it. "I've tracked down a distant cousin, but the owner of the house Maggie Morgan rented said the only belongings not given to charity were left with you."

"He didn't know what else to do with them. I didn't know what I was going to do with them, either. They're things that should go to family, to somebody who understands what they meant to her. But we didn't know of anyone like that, and it seemed terrible to throw out keepsakes. It would have felt like throwing her out, as if she didn't matter. And she did matter. To all of us." The woman paused a moment, staring off into space with sadness creasing her handsome features.

"So you did keep the things?" Logan prompted.

"They're in a box in our storeroom. I'll get them."

Janine Taylor went through a door behind her desk and, as Logan watched her go, he noticed several photographs on the wall on either side of the jamb.

The office was done in an elaborate and eclectic mixture of modern and antique furniture that somehow worked. But those particular pictures were simple snapshots—like family photos—hung as if for the sake of the staff rather than the customers.

Curious about them, Logan rounded the desk to have a look.

According to the snapshots, Designs Unlimited was apparently an award-winning firm. There were five photos of women smiling and holding plaques or statuettes.

The owner—Janine Taylor—was in all the shots, as were two more women, but the other faces changed from one picture to another.

Just then Janine Taylor returned carrying a half-empty case-size box plastered with a logo for russet potatoes on the side.

It didn't look heavy, but Logan took it from her, anyway, setting it on the seat of one of the chairs in front of the desk. He nodded toward the photos. "Is Maggie Morgan in any of those? I haven't come across a picture of her and I'd like to put a face with the name."

"Maggie is in the one on the bottom right. It was taken about two weeks before the accident."

Logan went back to have another look, and the designer joined him to point to her former employee. "That's her."

He leaned in to study Maggie Morgan.

She was not a head turner. In truth she was a very unremarkable-looking woman.

Her hair was wispy thin and an undistinguished pale shade of brown, pulled back into a librarian's bun. She wore very thick glasses that hid her eyes and were propped on a nose that was slightly too long. And she had large teeth, though it looked as if she'd practiced not to show too much of them when she smiled.

She was also the smallest woman in the picture, not only inches shorter than the rest, but also waifishly proportioned.

When he'd had his fill of studying the picture, Logan stood up straight again. "She looks nice."

"She was a sweetheart," Janine Taylor agreed. "One of the most genuinely kind and thoughtful people we've ever hired. Everyone liked her. She was easy to work with, easy to get along with, fun to have around—"

The woman's voice caught and Logan glanced at her as she hid tears in her eyes by leaving him and sitting in the chair behind her desk.

Logan went around and took a seat in front of it.

"We miss her," the woman added, having gained some control before the tears actually fell. "And we all feel very guilty."

"Why is that?"

She shook her head vehemently. "I know Madeline Van Waltonscot is your client, and maybe I shouldn't say this, but putting Maggie to work with her was...well, we've felt as if we threw a lamb to the wolves."

"Was Maggie Morgan that meek?"

"Not meek. Agreeable. It's what made her so easy to work with and such a success with clients. She could be open and honest about her views and opinions, advise people how to decorate their homes. But if the client didn't approve, she didn't take it personally or get upset and she never got pushy. She'd just go from there. We—my partners and I—thought her manner might make her the perfect match for Miss Van Waltonscot."

"That sounds reasonable. What's in it to make anybody feel guilty?"

"Part of why we let ourselves be convinced was that no one else wanted to work with the woman. We'd dealt with her before and none of us cared to repeat the experience. But the job meant a huge billing...."

She trailed off ashamedly, clearly having hit on what was causing everyone to feel guilty.

Only after a moment of sitting there silently did she go on, this time with the conviction of atonement. "We'll never work for Madeline Van Waltonscot again. I don't care how much money she has, it isn't worth it. She insisted that Maggie spend a full day with her, following her around like a shadow. She wanted Maggie to get a feel for her style, was how she put it. I told Maggie she didn't have to go, that she didn't need to play handmaiden to that prima donna if she didn't want to. We were doing a decorating job for her and that didn't have to go beyond showing her swatches and carting her around to furniture wholesalers. But Maggie said it was no big deal, that if it would make the woman happy—as if anything could make that shrew happy—she could spare just one day out of her life. Little did we know..."

That recounting was just what Maddie had told him, and unless Madeline Van Waltonscot had had this place bugged so she could overhear what was being said about her behind her back, Logan didn't know how she would have known this.

Still, he didn't want to be thinking things like that. So he changed the subject.

"Should I take it, since you still have Maggie Morgan's belongings, that she wasn't engaged or involved with anyone around here who would be interested in having some of her things?" Okay, so maybe he had a more personal reason for asking that question. But since it was already out, he listened intently for the answer.

"There wasn't anybody. We'd set her up on a few blind dates since she was new to Colorado and didn't know many people. But...well, she wasn't very pretty in the conventional sense and she didn't have a lot of luck with men. You all want a fashion model's face and body and overlook some terrific women who don't have them."

Logan smiled at her gentle rebuke. He hadn't always been above reproach on that score, as she'd clearly guessed. But it wasn't necessarily the rule, either.

"I don't know," he countered. "I've come across a woman or two who have a fashion model's face and body but such rotten personalities that they were easy to overlook."

"Your client for one."

Until now, anyway, he thought, only smiling in answer. But now his client's personality was different than it had been before. And he liked to think that if he'd encountered that same personality attached to Maggie Morgan's face and body, he'd have been just as attracted as he was reluctantly finding himself at the present.

But he needed to get back to business.

"Just out of curiosity," he said, adding a note of authority to his tone. "Did Maggie—or you or any of the other designers—ever meet a large man with a bent nose when you were with Miss Van Waltonscot or at her house?"

Janine Taylor's well-plucked eyebrows pulled together to let him know she thought his question odd. "Maggie was the only one of us to deal with Miss Van Waltonscot this time around, so none of the rest of us would have had occasion to be at her house or meet anyone connected to her."

"Did Maggie mention anyone? Or any unusual goings-on to do with Miss Van Waltonscot?"

"No. What does any of that have to do with locating Maggie's next of kin to return what's left of her belongings?"

"That isn't the only thing I'm working on for Miss Van Waltonscot. The accident left her with a few gaps in her memory that I'm also trying to help her fill."

"A few gaps in her memory," Janine Taylor repeated wryly. "Her carelessness killed one of the nicest people I've ever met and all she came out of it with was a few gaps in her memory. Somehow that doesn't seem fair."

"No, I don't suppose it does," Logan agreed. But he thought he'd learned all he was going to and stood to leave. "I appreciate you taking the time to talk to me and I'm sure Maggie Morgan's cousin will be glad to get her things."

She took one of her business cards from a silver salver on the corner of her desk and handed it to him. "Please send this along, too, and let the cousin know how sorry we all are and that if he—or is it she?"

"She."

"If she'd like to call and just talk about Maggie or what she was doing here or visit her grave, I'd be happy to talk to her or show her where she's buried."

That sparked another question in Logan's mind. "Who paid for her funeral?"

"There was no life insurance so the other designers and I all chipped in because we wanted her to have something nice. This is the first we've heard of a cousin and, believe me, we tried to track down some family."

"As I said, she's a very distant cousin."

"I suppose so distant it took a professional to find her."

"Right." Logan picked up the potato box and thanked the decorator again for her help.

Janine Taylor walked him to the door and held it open for him. "Good luck working for Madeline Van Waltonscot," she said as he went out. And then added under her breath, "You'll need it."

Logan silently agreed. But the luck he needed was not for what the woman thought.

It was for keeping a rein on his attraction to the new and improved Madeline Van Waltonscot. Who seemed to have a whole lot more of the traits Janine Taylor had just described as Maggie Morgan's, than those of the heiress.

BOARD MEETINGS, Maddie decided as she and Logan left the one they'd just attended, were not such horrible things after all.

Especially when she could attend them as the woman with all the power.

And get her nails done at the same time.

"Wow. Have you ever seen such a great manicure?" she marveled to Logan when they were back in his Jeep. "Although I did think an important business meeting was a weird place to have a manicurist waiting, didn't you?"

Logan glanced at her from the corner of his eye. "Uh-huh."

"So you had the feeling, too, that Madeline Van Waltonscot was meant to be seen and not heard, getting her nails done rather than actually participating?"

"Uh-huh."

"Then you probably didn't miss how unhappy all those suits were when I spoke up." But of all the suits in the boardroom, Logan looked the best in his navy blue pinstripe, and she'd almost been too distracted by that to pay attention.

"I don't know why they should have been so unhappy. You raised your hand and waited until you were called on before stepping on their biggest idea for increased profit margins."

Maddie laughed. "I guess I did look dumb raising my hand like a kid in a classroom."

"Not dumb but a little strange. Particularly when you happen to be the owner of the 783 stores they were discussing."

She was tired of splitting hairs over these things, so she didn't remind him that it was Madeline Van Waltonscot who owned them. Besides, technically now, the stores were hers. And it felt good to have stopped the implementation of a bad policy.

"I can't believe that with the huge profits already being made by Scottie's Food Marts, they would actually jockey employees around so hardly anyone works full-time and could qualify for benefits. Fat cats getting fatter at the expense of the little guy, that's all they were talking about, and I just couldn't *not* speak up," she said.

They were at a stoplight on the way to the Van Waltonscot house and Logan grinned over at her. "You surprised them, all right."

"For once I was glad to." She held up her hands again, fingers splayed. "And I got a terrific manicure in the process."

He laughed out loud at that, and the rich sound was like Belgian chocolate—smooth, tantalizing, leaving her wanting more....

Just in the nick of time he interrupted her wandering thoughts. "Did you tell the people who work at your house that I need to speak to them?"

"Everybody will be waiting when we get there." Maddie hesitated for a moment, wondering how to word the rest of what she had to say so that he wouldn't get the wrong idea. "And then I thought we could have dinner while we go through the things you brought from Designs Unlimited?"

He took his eyes off the road to glance at her.

"Not like a date or anything," she added in a hurry. "I just thought that by the time we got back and you asked your questions, dinner would be ready and it would just work out that you should stay. And besides, I owe you for being my moral support at that board meeting and—'' She was babbling. And wishing she were better at being coy.

She sighed and gave up the ghost. "The truth is that I can't tell you how much I hate sitting in that dining room with seventy-one empty chairs and that huge table stretched out in front of me, eating alone."

"And you're asking me to join you."

"I've tried changing the pattern. Taking a plate to my room. Setting things up in front of the television—more normal ways to eat by myself. But it seems to wound the chef—everything has to be served just so and in some sort of unimpeachable order, at the dining room table, only moments away from his preparation. And altering it gets everyone so upset that I don't have the stamina or the heart to go through with it."

"So that makes me the last alternative? After eating alone in your room or in front of the TV?"

Oh, sure, as if she weren't aching to have him stay, to have his company, to be able to look up from her plate to that gorgeous face of his, to hear that laugh again, to feel the heat of that gray gaze on her...

But she could hardly say that. Or actually admit it to herself since she wasn't even supposed to be having thoughts like that.

"The food is incredible," she enticed instead. "Four courses of things I usually can't pronounce but that are so delicious they'll make you cry." Of course he didn't need to know that what she was really craving was a hot dog smothered in chili, cheese and mustard.

"You're lonely," he said suddenly.

"It isn't as if I've found myself in a warm circle of friends," she conceded, realizing as she did, although she hadn't really considered it before, she supposed it was true. It was also true that even if she had been surrounded by friends and family, he'd still be the only one she was anxious to spend time with. But not under just any conditions, she thought when she saw clearly that he was suddenly feeling sorry for her.

"I'm not angling for a pity date, Strummel, so wipe that expression off your face."

"A pity date?" he repeated. "I thought this wasn't going to be a date at all. And I didn't know you were 'angling' for anything."

"I'm not. It only seemed like the courteous thing to do—asking you to stay for dinner."

"Oh, now you're just being polite, is that it?"

He was teasing her, she realized when she found him grinning at her again. "So are you going to do it or not?" she challenged, smiling back at him.

He pretended to think about it as he drove through the iron gates that opened to the bricked driveway that led up to the house.

But then he gave her an elaborate shrug and said, "Beats pretzels and beer in front of the tube at home."

"Smooth acceptance," she teased in return. "I'll try really hard not to be bowled over by your charm."

And not to be thrilled to death that what lay ahead of her was an evening with Logan.

MADDIE LEFT LOGAN ALONE to do his interview of the house staff, going upstairs to change clothes while he did.

In lieu of the jeans and T-shirt she would rather have climbed into, she opted for the most casual outfit she could put together—a pair of black stirrup pants she found in a drawer and a hot pink angora tunic sweater that was as soft as a cloud.

It was also slightly on the warm side for this early in autumn so she pushed the sleeves above her elbows.

Or maybe it wasn't the weather that was generating the heat. Maybe it was radiating from her, because her pulse was fast with excitement—and pleasure—more than it should have been at the prospect of the next couple of hours with Logan.

Once she was dressed she hung up the suit she'd had on before, buttoning all the buttons and smoothing it as carefully as if she'd just borrowed it for the occasion. Then she sat at the dressing table.

That first sight of herself in the mirror was still a jolt, but the shock waves were getting increasingly short-lived. And she was beginning to be secretly pleased with this new body and face. It almost seemed like one of those make-overs she was always seeing in magazines—only this one was a roaring success.

"In fact, you look like a whole new person," she joked to her reflection.

A whole new person whose appearance needed a lot less maintenance than the old one had.

She ran a brush through the long, silky hair that barely needed it and did a minor refreshing of the blush on cheekbones she'd only dreamed of having, and she was on her way.

When no one rushed out to ask if she'd like a cocktail this evening, Maddie knew Logan must still have everyone tied up in the kitchen. And since the table in the dining room hadn't been set yet, she decided to do that to keep herself busy.

Hunting through the four sideboards and three china cabinets for the dishes, glasses, linen napkins and silverware that were used every night took a while, and by the time she'd laid out a place setting at the head of the table and one around the corner from it, Logan came through the swinging doors to join her.

"Aha!" he said as if catching her in the act of something he'd only suspected her of before.

"Aha!" she responded the same way, feasting on the view of him in just his suit pants and dress shirt with the sleeves rolled to midforearm and the collar button open. Then she added, "'Aha' what?"

He took the glass she'd been about to put on the table out of her hand and set it down. Then he clasped both of her shoulders and steered her into the seat at the head of the table, whispering in her ear as he did, "These are the things that are driving your people crazy."

A shiver of delight skittered along her nerve endings from the feel of his strong hands and the warmth of his breath against her skin. Maddie couldn't do anything but wait for the sensation to subside before she could speak.

And it didn't pass until he released her to sit in the chair around the corner of the table.

"What things—" she whispered back, but that was as far as she got when one of the maids came through the door to the kitchen to ask if Maddie wanted dinner served now.

"What things are—" she tried again, but another young woman appeared with the soup course.

"Maybe the third time will be the charm," she said when they were finally alone again. "What things are driving what people crazy?"

Logan tested the soup, raised his eyebrows in approval, and in a louder, but still confidential voice said, "The lady of the manor does not set her own table. Or go into the kitchen to make her own tea and ask if anyone else would like a cup. Or lay out her own clothes or hang them up when she takes them off. Or shower rather than soak in legendary bubble baths while her personal assistant advises her of the day's schedule. Or reject two martinis before dinner every night in favor of lemonade. Or get up before eleven in the morning or eat breakfast anywhere but in bed."

He paused long enough to take another spoonful of soup and then went on. "The lady of the manor also should not need to be told that the television in her sitting room is behind a wall that moves with the push of a button. Or how to operate her shoe-selection system. Or how to work the intercom. Or—"

Maddie held up her hand. "In other words, I've gotten a bad report card."

"Not bad. It's just that since the accident everyone thinks that something is wrong with you. You seem awkward to them, you don't do the same things you did before and you're unfamiliar with what goes on around here."

There seemed to be a note of challenge in his voice, as if he were telling her what the staff had said about her to see what her reaction would be.

Her reaction was to answer him in the same quiet tone. "Well, what do you expect when I'm a stranger to it all?"

He only raised an eyebrow and Maddie sighed, wondering if he was ever going to believe her story.

She ate some of the soup, too, while Logan heaped praise on it. Then she said, "Did you leave out anything else I've confused people about? I better hear it all so I can try not to rock the boat anymore."

The soup bowls were taken away and the salads served before he started to give her a more complete version of the oddities the staff had found in her behavior during the past three weeks.

And by the time he finished they were nearly through the main course of broiled salmon fillets in dill sauce, angel-hair pasta with fresh tomato and basil and braised carrots—which Maddie despised, adding one more food that alerted the kitchen to her unusual new likes and dislikes.

"They think I'm nuts," she concluded after the chocolate mousse arrived.

"They think the accident shook you up more than anyone realized. That it knocked a few screws loose and that it would be good except they're all waiting for the pendulum to swing back at them."

"Which is why they're on pins and needles all the time, afraid for their jobs," she added, thinking about Bernice's fear over Maddie just wanting to dress herself.

"Basically, yes. Preaccident you never complained or changed anything without heads rolling for it."

"And I've been changing a lot—whether I knew it or not."

"Seems so." He'd been watching her intently all the while they were eating and talking, no doubt still curious about her response.

Or maybe he was finally beginning to see that she really wasn't who he thought she was.

"What about Bent Nose and the man on the answering machine? Does anyone know about either of them?"

"Zilch," he answered as he tasted the rich dessert that Maddie didn't have room for. "No one has seen

Bent Nose or knows anything about him. Your personal assistant—"

"Bernice."

"—has heard the messages on the answering machine but doesn't have any idea who the caller is. And no one knows what might be going on with either of them. Apparently it was a pretty hush-hush deal."

"Which makes it sound bad and you're probably back to being suspicious of me." Except that he didn't seem standoffish the way he had when he'd been suspicious before.

But he didn't answer her. After another moment of studying her, he pushed away from the table and stood.

"What do you say we check out the things in the box from Designs Unlimited?"

She got up, too, whispering to him as she did, "Good food, isn't it?"

"An odd comment coming from someone who, on the very morning of the accident, put the chef on notice that you weren't wild for his cooking."

"Oh Lord, no wonder the poor guy has been bending over backward every time I don't eat something." She glanced at the door to the kitchen. "And I left those carrots tonight. Maybe I should—"

Logan's hands came back to her shoulders the way they'd been before. Only this time he steered her out of the dining room and into the living room. "Reassure him tomorrow that he doesn't need to be looking for a new job. We have work to do."

But it wasn't work for Maddie, who anxiously led the way into the formal living room where the box of her belongings was on the floor in the center.

She went straight there and knelt beside it. "You don't know how glad I am that there's *something* left."

Not that there was much. Some family photographs in nice but inexpensive frames. A wedding album and another picture album. Bronzed baby shoes. An engraved nameplate. Some old letters tied up in faded satin ribbon. A manila envelope from which she took the battered purse and broken watch that had survived the accident. And a pressed corsage in a glass box.

Logan was sitting on the edge of the cushion of an armchair right beside her, elbows to knees, leaning forward to watch what she pulled out. He didn't make many comments, though, as she explained what everything was before setting it aside on the floor and going on to the next treasure. But when she held up the glass-boxed corsage, he said, "The first prom?"

Maddie shook her head and smiled at the memory. "The first Daughter's Day," she said. "My dad decided that since there was Mother's Day and Father's Day, I should have a day, too. The first Sunday in July. I was ten when the tradition started, and to commemorate it he bought me this corsage. The dog ate the one he got me the second year—here, there's a picture."

She picked up the all-purpose album, flipped through a few pages until she found what she was looking for and then pointed to the photo of a beagle with a rose petal poking out of one side of its mouth, making the dog look like a tango dancer.

"That was Bridget, our dog. By the fourth Daughter's Day—" Maddie turned a few more pages in the album and pointed to another picture "—I was embarrassed to have a corsage so I made him promise not to ever buy me another one." And the photograph proved just how much she hadn't liked that third gift because the young teenager in it was rolling her eyes and making a face while her father pinned it on.

"Kids just never appreciate some things," she said with a sad little laugh as she gave in to the urge to smooth her father's image with a single index finger as if to touch the man himself.

The sound of a small chuckle of his own made Maddie glance up at Logan.

He looked at her, back at the photo in the album, at the corsage in the glass box and then at her again. There was the strangest expression on his face—a combination of a frown and a sort of awakening, as if he were seeing her for the first time.

"You really are Maggie Morgan, aren't you?" he said after a moment, his deep voice quiet again, almost as though he were talking to himself.

Maddie smiled at him. "Only on the inside," she said, and for some reason tears sprang to her eyes. Hot, stinging tears that took her by surprise, flooding her view of him even as she swallowed back the lump in her throat and fought them.

Logan must have seen them, anyway, because he stood and pulled her up with him. Wrapping his arms around her, he held her pressed close to that big, broad chest of his, cupping the back of her head in one hand, rubbing a gentle thumb against her hair.

In the three weeks since Maddie had found herself in this predicament, in this body, no one had offered her comfort. No one had hugged her. No one had touched her in any way that wasn't perfunctory. No one had known—maybe not even she herself—how much she grieved for the part of herself that she'd lost.

He went on holding her closely, tenderly, letting his warmth and strength seep into her pores, renewing her in a way no doctor, no servants, no money or power could ever do.

But when his magic worked to dissolve the dark feelings she'd suppressed, something else replaced them. Something alive and sensual and wonderful.

Her own arms had found their way around Logan and her hands were against his back, but she hadn't realized it before. Now she suddenly became very aware of it. Of the feel of his broad shoulders and muscled back, the power in them.

His hand in her hair eased her head away from his chest, and those smoldering gray eyes delved into hers, searching, looking well past the surface for the first time.

Then he kissed her. Softly, chastely, almost as if he were reaching out to the woman she really was inside.

And he managed it, too. Touching the essence of Maddie, the spirit, the heart that she knew was her own.

But only for a moment. A brief moment before he ended that sweet kiss and put a little distance between them.

"This isn't a good idea," he said in a voice raspier than usual, letting her know he'd been as affected as she.

"No, it isn't," she agreed even as she tried to remember why.

"We have a job to do. A lot of things to sort through. Maybe some trouble to get you out of before it's too late."

"Right," Maddie agreed, widening the physical space he'd left by taking a step backward herself.

She could hear in his voice the struggle to return to business as he went on. "I think we better start tomorrow by going through this house—all of Madeline Van Waltonscot's things—with a fine-tooth comb. I don't suppose you've done that, have you?"

"I've only gotten into things I've absolutely had to," she confirmed.

"Well, hopefully we'll find something to get this show on the road."

She nodded and repeated, "Tomorrow," thinking that it would be much too long a time until she'd see him again but knowing she couldn't do anything about it.

"For tonight just get some sleep and we'll start fresh then," he ordered.

It made her laugh a little because sleep was tough to come by since he'd taken up residence in her thoughts. And in her desires. But she said, "Okay."

He ran just one index finger down the side of her face, as if he couldn't resist touching her again—or maybe to convince himself she was real—and said, "Good night, Maddie."

"Good night," she answered. And then she watched him cross the giant room and disappear into the foyer, truly ending the evening with the sound of the front door opening and closing behind him.

She fell back into the chair he'd been sitting on and blew out a long breath.

One wrinkle had been smoothed tonight, she knew, feeling the relief of finally having him believe that she was who she was. But a new wrinkle had been added, too.

In the form of a kiss.

And she couldn't help wondering if that new wrinkle might be even harder to iron out than the old one had been.

Chapter Four

Logan was a levelheaded, pragmatic, show-me kind of person who didn't even read his horoscope. So it wasn't easy for him to accept that the body of Madeline Van Waltonscot and the spirit, essence and intellect of Maggie Morgan had somehow been fused into one person—Maddie.

But as he drove to the Van Waltonscot estate the next afternoon he had a gut instinct that Maddie's story was the truth.

Of course, no matter how farfetched it seemed, she could have planted the jewelry in the hiding place at the rental house herself.

And she could be putting on an act with her house staff that made it look as if she were awkward and unfamiliar with her own home, her own schedule, her own likes and dislikes.

She could even have made up all the stories that went with the keepsakes in the box from Designs Unlimited—although she had seemed to know exactly what pictures were in that photo album and the pages they were on.

Despite what the skeptical realist in him could argue with, he seemed to be grasping at straws. The fact was, he just didn't doubt her anymore.

Last night Logan had suddenly been sure that the sweet, endearing, funny, guileless woman kneeling in front of him really wasn't Madeline Van Waltonscot.

Which hadn't helped him resist his attraction to her one damn bit.

Especially when he'd seen how lonely she really was, deep down inside. She didn't seem to have an ounce of self-pity, either, and his attraction to her had taken over and left him holding her, comforting her, kissing her, before he'd even thought about what he was doing.

She was still a client. She was still in the midst of something that was potentially illegal. And she was still a woman in one incredibly complicated situation, which, even in the event of the best possible conclusion, was going to leave her to deal with a whole new life.

He'd be out of his mind to get romantically involved with her under any one of those conditions, let alone all three.

And he wasn't out of his mind. Even though the power of whatever it was that was drawing them together made him feel as if he might be.

But no matter how terrific she was, no matter how nice or sexy or beautiful—inside and out—and no matter how many feelings she was stirring up inside of him, he had to keep his distance. He had to keep his head on straight. For his own sake and for hers.

Yet the closer he got to her house, to where he knew she waited for him, the more anxious he was, the more eager.

And no amount of reasoning seemed to help.

Because too vivid in his mind was a memory of his own . . .

Of holding that soft body of hers in his arms.

Of the smell of her hair.

The feel of her head against his chest.

The warm sweetness of her lips under his.

And, damn it all, he just wanted more of it.

AS SHE SHOWERED, Maddie was thinking about Logan's comment the night before that she was lonely.

It honestly wasn't something she'd contemplated since awakening from the coma—there had been too many other things on her mind—but his remark had brought the truth home to her.

Madeline Van Waltonscot might have lived with people around her twenty-four hours a day to do her bidding, but apparently not only didn't she have any family, she also didn't have any close friends or anyone who really cared about her.

With the exception of Bent Nose's single, furtive and brief visit at the hospital, no one else had so much as dropped by to say hello, not there or even at home since she'd been back.

A few cards and notes had arrived to wish her well now that she was on her feet again, but not one among them had been anything but dispassionate and dutiful.

Several large flower arrangements had been delivered with similar messages, though again, all from indifferent sources—The Sutly Family or The Women's Foundation or Your Friends at the Junior League—acquaintances at best, or groups or places the heiress probably donated money to.

And there were invitations to luncheons, to fashion shows, to functions for good causes, but even those were all formal and missing any kind of personal touch.

Even though she hadn't been in Denver all that long and really only knew the other decorators at Designs Unlimited, she didn't have a doubt that they'd have been at her bedside, calling her every day, stopping by, urging her to return to work and telling her how much they missed her.

And she missed them, she realized now.

Friendship. Companionship. Comfort in the aftermath of a terribly traumatic experience. Sharing her feelings and fears. Just plain talking, laughing, relaxing and having fun with people whose company she enjoyed and who enjoyed hers.

There hadn't been any of those things in this new life full of cold comforts.

Until Logan.

But was it Logan himself she was attracted to? Or was she just particularly vulnerable to *anyone's* kindness these days?

Unbidden, a picture of him popped into her mind's eye—the full six feet three inches of male-model perfection.

Not that being gorgeous was the only thing he had going for him, though. He had a quiet charm, too, that always made her feel she had his undivided attention. There was also an aura of competence and strength about him that made her know she was safe while he was around.

She recalled the moment when simple comforting had turned to more and remembered the feel of his mouth taking hers, the delicious agony of that kiss she'd wanted to go on and on.

In the three weeks since she'd awakened as the heiress, being with Logan was the best she'd felt.

Actually, being with Logan was the best she'd felt even before the accident.

Maybe, since fate seemed to have taken a major hand in her life already, she ought to give in to the attraction and trust that it was part of some grand design. The same way she had to hope the body exchange was.

Even if her relationship with Logan wasn't meant to be, she reasoned that being with him offered a sort of consolation for all she was missing by not having awakened as herself. Consolation that couldn't be found in money or the trappings of it. Consolation that just might be heaven-sent to replace some of what had been lost to her.

Except that kissing like they'd done the past two nights was definitely not something she'd have been getting as Maggie Morgan.

But the fact that she liked Logan—a lot—that she enjoyed his company, that she wanted to spend as much time with him as she could, was not something she was going to fight or try to talk herself out of anymore.

For the moment, at least, he filled a need she hadn't even known she had, and until things got settled, she wasn't going to turn her nose up at that. Or deny herself.

She was just going to be grateful for it. Draw from it. Try not to romanticize it. Which meant no more kissing.

If she could help it....

MADDIE WAS LISTENING for the doorbell when it rang or she wouldn't have heard it. She made a beeline out of her suite and did a quick skip down the stairs—as quick as sixty-four steps could be skipped down. She hoped that Logan wouldn't mind that she was wearing the freshly laundered jeans and navy blue shirt he'd loaned her the night they'd broken into the rental house.

She'd intended to return the clothes once they'd been washed, but when she'd gone into the closet to choose an outfit, there they'd been. And since she couldn't find anything more appropriate to wear for searching a house, she'd put them on.

"Hi!" she greeted him as she reached the last few stairs, at the same time one of the maids let him in.

"Hi, yourself," he answered.

She feasted on the sight of him as the maid closed the front door behind him.

He wore a pair of jeans and a red polo shirt, both of which fit him to perfection. The jeans were just tight enough to skim his hips and muscular thighs, the shirt was loose around his narrow middle, but swelled to the breadth of his chest and shoulders. The sleeves were pulled tight across biceps that Maddie's hands suddenly itched to explore, and the top two out of three buttons were left open around his thick, powerful-looking neck.

No question about it, the man was definitely to-die-for.

"I hope you don't mind that I'm wearing your clothes again," she said when the maid had left them alone. "I really am going to return them. In fact, I was thinking of making you a proposition to get myself some replacements."

That hadn't come out quite the way she'd meant it to, and the one-sided smile on Logan's supple mouth told her he knew it but wasn't likely to let her off the hook.

His gray eyes went from the top of her head to her feet and back again. "You look great in the clothes, but propositioning your way out of them? Isn't that a little drastic?"

"Not the kind of a proposition you mean," she reprimanded playfully. "I was thinking that maybe we could do a little shopping for some casual clothes of my own, and if you'd pay for them you could add it to the statement you send—along with a little extra for your trouble. Then Bernice will forward it to the accountant, who will pay you in full, and that way I'll have a couple of pairs of jeans and some regular shirts for days like today."

"Planning to do a lot of house searches, are you?"

"No, I just don't seem to have any knock-around clothes."

"Who are you thinking of knocking around?"

"Come on, you know what I mean," she objected even though she was enjoying his banter. There was something different about him today, less business-like, more friendly.

He looked her up and down again, this time with an assessing lift of one eyebrow. Then he nodded. "You do look good in a pair of blue jeans. It'd be a shame not to see you in them more often."

His compliment sent a little thrill along the surface of her skin. She tried to ignore it. "I still feel sort of funny about spending Madeline Van Waltonscot's money even this way, but—"

"Think she's coming back?"

"No, that never even occurs to me. I saw her disappear into the light."

"The light?"

"Long story."

"Mmm. Well, save it for later then. But as far as I can tell, with the body and the life came the money, Maddie. The whole kit and caboodle are yours. So why feel guilty about spending some of it?"

"It just seems weird, that's all. Especially when I have to use subterfuge to get myself some blue jeans. It seems like stealing."

"It isn't, though."

"Well, anyway, maybe today we'll come across a stash of cash earmarked for me. Then I can use that and I won't need to involve you."

"I don't mind," he assured her amiably. "But somewhere down the line you might try saying the accident left your motor skills altered and that's why your signature looks different now. I'm sure you won't have any problem getting new credit cards issued, and the bank will no doubt make all the allowances you need on any accounts for Madeline Van Waltonscot."

She pretended to be shocked, even as she reveled in this more relaxed Logan Strummel, who apparently really did believe her now. "Are you aiding and abetting me?"

"Guess I am. Again. And why not? It's too late to pull out now."

"Okay, then. First the searching, then the shopping. Shall we start upstairs in my room?"

"Now that does sound like a proposition," he teased her, maybe not as innocently as she'd thought.

"In your dreams, Strummel," she countered.

He grinned and swept an arm toward the stairs. "After you."

As Maddie headed back the way she'd come, she said, "I've already gone through the clothes drawers and the closet and didn't come up with anything." She'd made sure to do it herself that morning because she hadn't wanted him to search through all that sexy, lacy underwear.

"Did you take the drawers all the way out, check the bottoms, the sides, the backs, to make sure nothing was taped to them?"

Chagrined, she said, "No, I didn't think to look in any of those places."

"How about inside all the pockets of the clothes, inside all the shoes, the purses, anything and everything there's an inside to?"

Again she grimaced at her own oversight. "Nope."

"Looks like we'd better do it again, then."

So much for trying to circumvent anything.

She led the way into the closet and stepped to one side so he could join her. When he did, he paused and glanced around the whole large space, somewhat slack jawed. "And you don't have enough to wear?"

She laughed. "Amazing, isn't it? I didn't say I don't have enough to wear, but believe it or not, in all of this stuff there isn't a single pair of blue jeans or a plain old T-shirt."

"Who'd need them?"

"Me."

That made him laugh a little, though she didn't know why. But rather than enlightening her, he merely shook his head and pointed to the built-in dresser drawers. "Might as well start there."

But "there" was where the underwear waited, and it took Maddie a moment of shoring up her courage to follow him.

Not that she needed it.

He was all business from then on, searching more thoroughly than she would ever have known to do and teaching her as he did.

The closet was the biggest job and they emptied every purse and checked out every pocket and shoe, every hatbox and nook and cranny of the space. After that her private office and the rest of the suite were a breeze.

Then they moved on to the remainder of the house, which was easier still since the other two top-floor suites were as empty of personal effects as the guest rooms on the second level.

The first floor was no small task, but even though they emptied innumerable drawers and generally turned each room inside out, at the end of the day what little they had to show for their work had still come from Maddie's rooms.

As they shared another feast of an evening meal, Logan laid it all on the table in front of them. They'd struck gold in the form of the heiress's day planner, which contained her checkbook, credit cards, address book and calendar.

They'd also unearthed two unsigned notes in a shoe box in the very back of the closet. One said, "Relayed refusal and message to leave you alone." The other said, "Gave second warning and did some vandalizing to let them know we mean business." But neither of the notes bore anything that could be used to trace them to the sender.

"Those don't make things look good," Maddie said in reference to them. "Unless they're from Bent Nose and he's been hired to get someone to stop doing something bad to Madeline Van Waltonscot, then maybe that means she wasn't doing anything illegal, after all, but just trying to protect herself."

"Mmm," Logan murmured noncommittally. "Except that vandalizing is still vandalizing and that *is* illegal."

"Maybe it's not as bad as it sounds, though. Maybe whoever he'd warned is really awful and dangerous and didn't pay attention to the first message, so Bent Nose had to do something more drastic. And if whoever he's warning was doing something illegal to begin with, wouldn't that make it sort of justifiable?"

"Did the guy on the answering machine sound to you like somebody doing something so rotten he deserved whatever he got?"

"No. He sounded like somebody having something undeservedly bad done to him," she admitted.

Logan didn't respond. He only set the notes aside and pulled the day planner close enough for them both to look through as they ate.

The checkbook ledger wasn't much more revealing than the notes had been. Clearly the accountant did take care of the bills because the heiress wrote very few checks, mainly to stores. But there were three large amounts written to cash—one of them dated just the day before the accident. Since they hadn't come across much money to show for it, Logan guessed they were payments to Bent Nose.

"Which adds points to the illegal column," Maddie conceded. "Otherwise, if what Bent Nose is doing is okay, she'd have just made the check out to him by name, wouldn't she have?"

"It's a possibility," Logan confirmed. "Or it could be she just spent all that cash right away and Bent Nose's services are being billed to the accountant like everything else, all on the up-and-up."

He flipped to the notepad portion of the personal organizer. Many of the notes written there were to remind the accountant to pay expenses Madeline Van Waltonscot had incurred and make whatever donations she'd promised—promises she apparently didn't make kindly since she referred to some of the fund-raisers as "money grubbers" who had "badgered" her into the contributions.

The rest were reminders of appointments, and a few were notations to herself to level formal complaints to have salespeople fired for being rude to her or not doing their job the way she thought they should.

From there they went through the address book, finding the accountant's name, address and telephone number, as well as that of the heiress's law firm.

The rest of the entries were ordinary. Businesses, organizations, groups, foundations, some of Denver's most distinguished citizens.

Lastly they went through her calendar, finding the initials *H.D.* and *3:00 p.m.* penciled in on one day. It might not have seemed odd, except that every other notation had a full name written out, along with a brief reminder such as luncheon or dental appointment or hairdresser or fitting, while this had nothing like that.

"Not much to go on," Maddie said when they'd covered the whole day planner.

Logan grinned at her. "What did you expect? That we'd look under *B* and find Bent Nose, Thug for Hire, listed?"

She smiled back. "It would have been nice."

"We didn't do too badly. Tomorrow we can pay a visit to the accountant and the lawyer, ask a few questions, get a copy of whatever wills are in effect— Madeline Van Waltonscot's, if there is one, and whatever it took for her to inherit all she did."

"You think this is over her inheritance? Or maybe what she could leave to someone else?"

"Money brings out the worst in people. And when there's as much involved as there is here, we can't discount that someone might have felt they should have gotten a share of it, or should when she dies. Then, too, there's blackmail, although that would be harder to trace through a lawyer or an accountant. But they're places to start, anyway. Plus, if we see the accountant, I'm betting he'd be the man to do whatever it takes to accommodate a change in your signature on credit cards and checks."

Maddie nodded, appreciating his help and ideas. Among other things.

"I can also get him to reimburse you for whatever I spend tonight."

"Don't worry about that."

They'd finished eating by then, and she was anxious to go shopping so she suggested they get to it.

Logan folded the notes and put them in one of the compartments of the day planner. "We should keep this handy since it's basically all we've got."

But as he said that and began to close it, a slip of paper they'd overlooked dislodged from somewhere inside of the organizer and floated to the table.

"What's this?" Maddie mused, picking it up to find a phone number on it. No name. No address. Just a number.

Logan studied it, did a quick scan through the address book for one that matched it but didn't find anything.

"So it could be a lead!" Maddie said excitedly.

"Could be."

"But you don't sound convinced. What else would a single piece of paper, hidden away in the planner, with only an anonymous phone number on it be?"

He laughed at her excitement. "Just about anything."

"But it could be a lead."

"Yes, it could be."

"So what are we going to do about it?" she asked as if top-secret documents had just fallen into their hands.

"How about dial the number and see who answers?"

Maddie didn't waste any time bringing him the phone, which was on one of the sideboards and was contained in an oak box that looked as if it should hold expensive cigars.

She kept her eyes and ears trained on Logan as he dialed, but after a long moment he hung up again without having said anything.

"No answer," he explained. "But there's another way to check it out," he said, as if to reinflate her appetite for the intrigue of it all. Which it did.

"How?" she demanded eagerly. "And if you say to keep calling until someone answers, I'm going to punch you."

He laughed. "A reverse phone book. It'll list the numbers in order and give us the name and address of who it belongs to."

"Great! Where do we get one?"

Logan didn't answer. Instead he made another phone call, this one to someone who sounded like a friend. And when it ended he said, "We're all set. First shopping and then to the police station when the night shift starts. I have a buddy who'll let us use the reverse directory there."

"Ooh, now this is getting interesting," Maddie nearly whispered, as if no one should overhear.

Logan rolled his eyes at her at the same time his mouth gave her a smile that said he was enjoying her. "Let's just hope it'll get us more information," he said as he picked up the organizer and ushered her out of the house.

SHOPPING WAS EASY ENOUGH once Maddie discovered what sizes fit her new body. She came away with three pairs of blue jeans, a pair of black ones, a chambray shirt, a pink-and-tan plaid blouse and two turtleneck T-shirts. She also bought a pair of desert boots and a package of men's undershirts—extra-large—to sleep in.

"Now I feel like I can tackle anything," she confided as Logan carried her packages out to his Jeep.

And yet she was going to hate giving back his shirt after it had been laundered again because she liked the feel of something that belonged to him wrapped around her. Not that she wanted to admit that. Even to herself.

It was nearly ten by the time they got to the police station in downtown Denver. Of the uniformed officers they passed on their way through the building, only about half of them greeted Logan with any sort of friendliness. And even most of those seemed to do so furtively, as if they didn't want to be caught fraternizing with him.

If Logan noticed—and Maddie didn't know how he couldn't have—he didn't comment on it. Maddie found it all very curious and began to wonder under what conditions he'd left the force.

Even Jerry Duke, the buddy he'd called earlier, looked around before closing Logan and Maddie into a private office.

But just as Maddie was about to ask why Logan seemed to be such a pariah around there, the tall, heavyset policeman came back with the reverse directory.

He stayed long enough to exchange a few amenities, then left them to the phone book and the computer terminal on a table at one side of the room.

Since Logan seemed more inclined to get to work than to talk, Maddie saved her questions for later.

"Harry Denton," Logan announced when he'd looked up the telephone number. "He lives in Thornton. Here—" he handed her the day planner they'd brought with them "—write this down."

Maddie turned to the notepad and he dictated the information.

"He's listed as a detective," Logan finished.

That raised Maddie's eyebrows. "A detective? Like a police detective?"

"Private, I'm sure. I don't know any police detectives who use the title in the phone book."

"So this guy is a detective as in Strummel Investigations detectives, then."

"Only Strummel Investigations wouldn't do what this guy may be doing." Logan went on to explain about Madeline Van Waltonscot having tried to hire his brother for something that hadn't sounded as if it were on the level.

"So you think she found Harry Denton instead," Maddie concluded. "And that he's the *H.D.* on the calendar."

"Seems possible. Does that name ring any bells?" he asked as he closed the directory.

"Not for me. Does it for you?"

Logan shook his head.

"The name isn't listed in the address book," Maddie said when she'd checked the heiress's entries.

"Guess they didn't exchange Christmas cards. Let's plug him into the computer and see if he has a record," Logan suggested, going to the machine.

Maddie pulled a chair to sit beside him in front of it as he punched in the necessary codes to access what he needed.

"Nope. Harry Denton has a slew of unpaid parking tickets from all over the city, but no record."

"Any information on who he is?"

"Not from parking tickets—they're usually issued without the person being anywhere around, which means the vehicle information is all that's available in the system."

"I guess that means it doesn't say if he has a bent nose or not, huh?"

"Unbelievable what's omitted, isn't it?" he said, playing along.

"What about his occupation? If he's a P.I., doesn't he need a license or something and wouldn't there be a record of it?"

"The state of Colorado doesn't require a license to be a P.I. Anybody can hang out a shingle and claim the title."

"Oh. Then even some creep who'd do bad things to people could call himself a detective."

"Afraid so."

"Well, at least now we have a name and address. That's something," she said with a sigh.

But Logan wasn't ready to abandon this tack yet. "Let's try a couple of other things and see what we come up with."

The screen went blank, and then he brought up some different files, explaining as he did. "We can check for reports of harassment and see if Madeline Van Waltonscot's or Harry Denton's name comes up. And we can check into any recent vandalism, see if we find anything."

Maddie watched intently, but when the computer had completed its search they didn't know anything they hadn't before.

"Okay. How about Madeline Van Waltonscot," he suggested as he typed in the name. "One D.V.I.— charges dropped. One reckless-driving citation—the date of the accident—charges dropped."

"How can that be? She was responsible for a death and didn't even get a ticket?"

"Money, power, connections, social position, Maddie. And a damn good lawyer who fixed things even while his client was lying in a coma. Be glad or you'd be facing a hornet's nest for what she did."

That was true. The reminder cooled her sense of outrage and brought her back to matters at hand. "I don't suppose there's any mention of her being involved in some way with a guy named Harry Denton?''

Logan shook his head. ''Just the two tickets, nothing else. Except . . .'' He punched in some other commands, and different information came up on the screen. ''Not coincidentally, at the same time as both citations, Madeline Van Waltonscot became a very, very generous contributor to some programs that are near and dear to every cop's heart. The college-scholarship fund for kids of cops. The fund to help families of cops killed in action. The Dare to Keep Kids off Drugs program—''

''Which is how she got away with—'' Maddie had almost said murder, but it seemed too extreme a statement, so she amended it ''—with not having the tickets upheld.''

''Mmm,'' Logan agreed. Then he glanced at her out of the corner of his eye and smiled devilishly. ''How about Miss Maggie Morgan? I wonder if we have anything on her.''

''Only if there's a file on model citizens.''

''In borrowed bodies.''

''Hey! This body better not just be a loaner. It better be a keeper or I'm in bigger trouble than we thought.''

''Yep. Here it is. She's wanted for body snatching in seventeen states.''

Maddie slapped his arm playfully, wishing she weren't so aware of the hardness of his biceps even in such contact. ''Very funny. What's really there?''

''I'm afraid you're only a statistic, love. Auto-accident fatality.'' He looked straight at her. ''Good thing we know better.''

She smiled at him, grateful for that vote of confidence, and tried not to be pleased by the endearment that he'd probably only intended to cushion what he was saying.

But he grinned back at her, and for a moment his shining gray eyes held hers, compounding the effect. But more than the word or the look, she had the sense of a new closeness between them, a closeness that sent a heat wave through her that nearly melted her insides.

And then the door opened and Jerry Duke poked his head in, interrupting the moment.

"I have to answer a domestic disturbance. You about through? I'd hate to have somebody find you in here when I'm not around to run interference."

Logan exited the computer program. "All set."

"Great, then come on and I'll walk out with you guys."

The other man said it as if they needed his escort, but Logan didn't seem to notice that, either. He turned off the computer, took the day planner in one hand and Maddie's elbow in the other.

Just that simple touch was enough to keep her occupied on the way out as Logan and Jerry Duke made small talk. It sent tiny bolts of lightning up her arm and left her fighting hard against liking the silent possessiveness it relayed.

And then they were back at his Jeep. He handed her up into the passenger seat and let go.

Very disappointing. Maddie suffered the loss in silence during the five minute drive to the Van Waltonscot estate and then realized with a jolt as Logan parked in front of the house that if she didn't do something in a flash he was going to go home.

"How about a midnight snack?" she suggested. "I build a great sandwich."

He hesitated a moment, and she knew he was debating the wisdom of staying after the way things had ended the night before. She could almost hear him telling himself that sending her up to her door alone right now was the smartest, safest thing to do.

But apparently he didn't want to leave any more than she wanted him to go because he said, "You're on," and grabbed her packages from the back seat to carry them in.

The front door opened before they'd even reached it, and a weary-looking maid welcomed them home.

Maddie had repeatedly told Bernice to let the staff know that no one had to be on call through the night, but clearly that change hadn't been taken seriously.

"You don't need to wait up anymore," Maddie was quick to tell the maid, sending her off to bed. Then, over her shoulder to Logan as she led the way to the kitchen, she said, "Now to tackle the assistant chef."

The chef himself didn't live in, but his assistant had the first set of rooms in the staff wing, right off the kitchen. And every time Maddie had sneaked downstairs for a late-night cup of tea or snack, the younger of the two men had come out in his bathrobe to insist on preparing it for her.

Which was just what he did now, within moments of Maddie's turning on the light in the expansive, blindingly white kitchen.

"It's okay, John. We're just going to fix a bite to eat. Go on back to bed."

The poor guy didn't seem to know what to do, but after gently arguing with him, Maddie managed to convince him she wanted to do it herself.

"See how it is?" she said to Logan when the other man had finally retreated. "It's very strange to have to fight over letting yourself into the house or just making your own food."

Logan shrugged and sat on a bar stool at the marble counter while Maddie set out bread, lunch meat, cheese and condiments and went to work assembling them. "Maybe you should sit back and enjoy being waited on."

"Makes me feel guilty," she confided. "And lazy and much too self-indulgent."

"Somehow that sounds like the minister's daughter talking."

"I guess the body is easier to shed than the values are." She paused a moment and then went on as she slid a dish with his sandwich on it in front of him. "I'd think it would be hard to stop being a cop, too. There must be a lot of that that gets ingrained pretty deeply."

"Bone deep, yeah."

"So why did you quit?" Maddie took a bite of her sandwich and watched him laugh a small, wry laugh.

"Noticed how things were at the station and it made you curious, didn't it?"

She shrugged. "I couldn't help noticing. It wasn't as if you got a warm reception."

He shrugged again. "Being a cop is like being in a private club, a fraternity. There's a brotherhood to it, unspoken codes that hold it together and close the ranks. When someone breaks those codes, things have a tendency to fall apart."

"And you broke a code? I find that hard to believe."

"I broke the blue wall of silence—the code that says cops protect other cops, cover for them, keep their mouths shut about them or what they do."

"No matter what they might do?"

"Some say yes. And in a lot of instances I agree. It isn't an easy job and sometimes rules have to be broken, limits stretched, slack given. But when you run into a cop who's doing more than that, who's crossed the line into criminal activity of their own, well, I couldn't just keep quiet and let it go on."

"Of course you couldn't. I wouldn't think any cop could." Maddie was less interested in eating than in Logan and concentrated on the play of emotions crossing his face as he spoke. "Can I know what happened?" she asked gently.

He shrugged one of those broad shoulders. "It isn't a secret. There was a cop who'd been on the force twenty-some years, well liked, well connected—his brother-in-law had the ear of the police commissioner, no less. Anyway, I got partnered with Drummond when both of our usual partners were out on leave. And I caught him taking bribes, big money, to look the other way on drug deals. One of those deals led to a murder, which was how I had my eyes opened about him and when I felt I had to bust him, cop or not."

"It seems to me that there should have been some sort of commendation for that."

He shook his head and seemed to lose his appetite, too, sliding the dish away and leaning on his forearms on the counter. "The blue wall of silence is a code of loyalty among the people who are supposed to be the good guys. This was a deal where one of the good guys looking the other way meant one of the bad guys—

and the guy who was killed was a bad guy—died. So, yes, there were some, no small number, who thought I was doing worse to go after the cop than the cop had done by taking a payoff to let it happen."

"But you did it anyway."

"I didn't become a cop so I could sit back and watch other cops commit crimes."

The harshness in that reply told her how difficult it had been for him to do what he'd felt was right. "So you busted him and then quit the force?"

"Not quite. I busted him and it ruined my career. That's when I found out about his connections to higher-ups. Plus my captain happened to be one of the people who believed the wall of silence shouldn't have been broken. That I should have just left it to him to reprimand Drummond—which would have meant nothing but a slap on the wrist—and kept my mouth shut."

"Instead you treat the guy the way you would have any other criminal and they fired you for it?"

"They didn't fire me for it, no. But the career I'd wanted for myself suddenly dried up. The only duty I pulled was what everyone knew I didn't want—desk duty, parade patrol, assignments for security for visiting dignitaries, rock stars, high profile bigwigs. I wasn't a cop, I was a secretary and security guard."

"And that wouldn't suit you at all," Maddie agreed.

"I tried transferring out of the department, into someplace where I'd at least have my immediate superiors on my side, but I was basically blacklisted. That left my only option IA."

"IA?"

"Internal Affairs. Cops investigating cops, a lot of the time for things that *should* be left alone. They call it the rat squad."

"Not a highly thought-of job, I take it."

"Not by a lot of cops. Not by me," he answered simply enough, but the disgust in his tone told more of the story.

"So you resigned. Even though you'd really rather still be a cop."

"Being a P.I. is the next best thing. Better in some ways because I'm my own boss." He grinned genuinely again, as if the darker feelings about what had gone wrong in his career had passed. "And I get to meet up with women who've 'seen the light.'"

"Yes, you do," Maddie confirmed.

"But exactly what light is it you've seen?"

Clearly he was changing the subject and the serious tone they'd lapsed into. But Maddie knew all she needed to about what had happened to him and didn't mind. "*The* light," she answered.

"Tell me about it."

She did, for the first time voicing what had happened to her when she'd found herself in that dark tunnel, looking down into the emergency room. "Madeline Van Waltonscot went into the light, and I wanted to, but I just couldn't move. And then I was sort of pulled down—kicking and screaming, in my mind, anyway—into the wrong body."

He nodded as if he understood. "After that first day when you came to hire me I went to the library and checked out some books on near-death experiences. They're all pretty much what you're describing. Except, of course, that people who claim to have done it return to their own bodies."

"Instead of being switched at birth, I was switched at death."

"I keep wondering if there's a reason for it."

"You and me both. Or if it really is just a big cosmic joke."

He studied her, looking into her eyes again, as if for answers. Then, very quietly, he said, "I can't believe it's just a cosmic joke."

She laughed. "How about that it's part of some grand design? I sort of go back and forth between the two."

"And what would the grand design be?"

"Good question. I keep wondering that myself."

"To right some wrong Madeline Van Waltonscot did?" he suggested.

"That seems the most likely, doesn't it? Especially in view of Bent Nose and the notes and the messages on the answering machine."

"Or maybe because we were supposed to meet, and at the last minute someone realized that hadn't happened yet and sent you back in the only vessel available," he said with melodramatic overtones as he stood to go.

"And together we're supposed to right wrongs," she added in the same vein, following him to the foyer. "The Near-Death Duo—maybe it'll end up as a TV series."

He turned to her at the door, and though he was smiling, it wasn't a joking kind of smile anymore. It was softer than that. Tender. Searching. "Maybe you were sent back for more personal reasons."

"Such as?"

"Such as to stir things up in me and make me have feelings I shouldn't be having."

"Ah, you think I'm here to torture you," she teased to make light of this suddenly more serious mood.

"Or reward me?" he suggested with a hint of a devilishly delicious grin that teased again.

But there was nothing teasing in the hand he reached to her cheek, drawing her as if by magic nearer to him as he delved into her eyes with his. And Maddie went willingly, giving in to the pull of that magnetic man and her own feelings for him.

He captured her mouth with his in a kiss that was firm, gently forceful, staking a claim to her, almost branding her with the heat of it.

And Maddie welcomed it all, melting against that big body of his with one hand at the hard, muscled mound of his pectoral, savoring the mastery of his kiss, the feel of his body so close, the leashed power that emanated from him.

His lips parted and urged hers to do the same so his tongue could find its way to hers to do a little circle dance that sent shivers down her spine.

But Maddie met him and matched him, eager to learn the steps he was teaching, the tastes and textures of him, the delights.

His arm was wrapped around her, holding her, while the other hand still cupped her face, slowly tracing her jawline with his thumb in sensual strokes that set off sparks there, too, as only his touch could.

Maddie's head was far back, her eyes closed. Kissing him at that moment seemed as necessary as breathing and she couldn't give it up.

Yet, all too soon, he ended it.

Not abruptly, but with a few farewell flicks of his tongue, two short, chaste kisses on her mouth and one on the tip of her nose.

"There has to be a reason, Maddie," he whispered, and she knew he meant not only a reason she was sent back here, but also a reason they'd met, a reason for what was happening between them in spite of everything.

"I guess we just have to wait and see what it is," she whispered back a bit dreamily because she was still well within the rapture of those kisses they'd just shared.

"I guess we do," he agreed.

Then he kissed her one last time, quickly, and slipped out the door.

But even once he was gone, her pulse still raced, her skin felt as if it were aglow, her mouth tingled to remind her of those last moments together.

And in his wake she knew that she was kidding herself to think that what she felt for that man was anything at all like simple friendship.

Chapter Five

"Lindsey! What are you doing here?" Logan greeted his sister when he went in the back door of the main house around noon the next day and found her having coffee with Quinn at the kitchen table.

"I have to testify in court on a case I investigated a few months ago and I need my notes," the youngest of the Strummel offspring explained.

Logan wrapped an arm around her shoulders and kissed the top of her head, then let go of her to pour himself a cup of coffee and join them at the table, giving her the once-over as she fluffed her dark, waifishly cut hair. Her delicate-featured face was luminous, her silver eyes sparkling with happiness.

"You look great. Is this the honeymoon glow or does being a wife and mother again just agree with you that much?" he asked.

She gave him a radiant smile. "Well, since I've been married for all of a week, I guess this could be called the honeymoon—even though we're only trying to merge households rather than take a trip and I can't avoid spending this afternoon in court. But being a wife and mother again definitely agrees with me. Graham is a terrific guy and the twins are so adorable

I can hardly take my eyes off them. So who can say what's making me glow?''

She nudged Logan's shin with the toe of her flat shoe where he sat across from her and Quinn. "What about you? I expected to find you mourning your resignation from the force, and instead you're bright eyed and bushy tailed and more chipper than I've seen you in months."

Logan caught Quinn frowning at him but responded to their sister. "I guess being a private investigator agrees with me."

"Or the client does," Quinn muttered under his breath.

"Who's the client?" Lindsey asked.

"Madeline Van Waltonscot," Quinn answered before Logan could, and with a throat full of disdain, which raised Logan's hackles and made him feel protective.

"Maddie," he amended pointedly.

This time Quinn's eyebrows shot up at him. *"Maddie,"* he mimicked the affectionate tone that had crept into Logan's voice. "Let me guess, you're starting to believe that wild tale of hers."

"Believe what wild tale?" This from Lindsey.

Logan filled her in on the case and the circumstances of it, then brought them both up-to-date—confessing that, yes, he had come to believe Maddie's story along the way, and why.

"You have to admit, Quinn," he said when he was finished, "that you saw a big change in her that day the two of you ran into each other here."

"A near-death experience that went awry and landed one person in another person's body, Logan?" Quinn said dubiously, admitting nothing.

"The library has books on near-death experiences. Studies have been done all over the world on people who've had them and relay exactly the same kind of story Maddie tells. And the fact that she ended up in another body? I'll grant you that is harder to swallow. But I've seen and heard too many things to doubt it anymore. And the one thing I haven't seen so much as a hint of is the old Madeline Van Waltonscot. Neither has a single one of her house staff—people who know her better and more intimately than you or I, and who've gotten a concentrated dose of the new Maddie since the accident."

"I don't suppose the fact that you're attracted to her has any bearing?" Quinn said as if he were cutting to the heart of the matter.

"Oh no, not another one of us falling for a client," Lindsey muttered.

But Quinn never took his eyes off Logan. "Are you 'falling' for her?"

"That doesn't have anything to do with it."

"So you are," Lindsey surmised.

Logan wished he could deny it, but how could he when it was the truth? He just couldn't help himself. But even if he couldn't help himself or deny it, he didn't want it to be a factor in Quinn or Lindsey's consideration of the case, because he honestly felt sure it wasn't a factor in his.

"My feelings for Maddie are completely separate from what she hired me to do. But I will tell you this, what I feel for her comes from getting to know the person she is now, and it's in spite of her having three strikes against her from the beginning. Strike one, I couldn't stand the preaccident Madeline Van Waltonscot. Strike two, I didn't believe this incredible body-exchange story any more than you do, Quinn. And strike three, I thought she was either trying to run a scam on me or had more than a few screws loose."

"And none of that is true now?" Quinn asked.

"No," Logan said simply, in his firmest cop voice.

"Logan is no dummy, Quinn," Lindsey put in. "No matter how far-out this sounds, if he thinks there's some validity to it, then maybe there is."

Quinn was still watching him, and Logan returned the stare, eye to eye.

Finally his brother shook his head. "I'm just worried about you. Leaving the force was a big hurdle, a major change in your life. Times like that leave us all a little off balance. A little vulnerable."

"Thanks for the concern," Logan answered, meaning it. "But I'm doing all right. Really."

Quinn nodded. "I hope so. But be careful, anyway."

"I will be," Logan assured. Then he turned the conversation to business. "Either one of you ever hear of a guy named Harry Denton?"

Quinn and Lindsey exchanged a look before Lindsey answered. "He's a P.I. The kind that give us a bad name."

"Is that who Madeline Van Waltonscot hired for whatever it was she wanted me to handle a few months ago?" Quinn asked.

"I don't know. We found his phone number tucked away in her day planner. Seems like a possibility."

"The guy is bad news," Lindsey said ominously.

"How come he doesn't have a record?" Logan asked. "Because I ran a check on him and he doesn't."

"Probably because he just hasn't been caught at anything yet," Quinn said. "He hasn't been around here long. Not even a year, I don't think. He came in from California."

"We butted heads with him in a child-custody case he claimed was his first job when he got here," Lindsey explained. "We were working for the mother, investigating the father. When the father realized what we were doing, he hired Denton to make the mother look bad so she'd lose her kids."

Quinn took up where she'd left off. "The mother was clean, so Denton started making things up. When we disproved them he tried to buy us off."

"Nice." Logan took his coffee cup to the sink, rinsing it and putting it in the dishwasher.

Quinn frowned at him again when he came to stand behind the chair he'd previously been sitting in. "Whatever you do, don't let your client meet with him on her own. He's not above turning the tables on her, either."

"When we refused to take his payoff," Lindsey filled in, "he hinted that he wasn't opposed to sharing some things he knew about his own client. For the right price."

"And," Quinn added, "if Madeline Van Waltonscot starts in with some story about not remembering him, he's liable to turn mean."

"Don't worry. I didn't have the slightest intention of letting her see him alone." Logan didn't add that these days there wasn't anything he wanted Maddie to do without him, though thinking she was in danger wasn't the reason. It was his feelings for her that were ruling. He just plain wanted to spend every minute with her himself. But Quinn didn't need to know just how bad off he was.

"Well, I'll keep you guys informed," he said. "Right now I'm going to pick her up so we can pay a visit to her accountant and her lawyer."

Logan squeezed his sister's shoulder as he passed behind her chair. "Happy honeymoon, such as it is."

She laughed. "Thanks."

To Quinn he said, "Say hello to Cara."

Quinn nodded just once. "Be careful, Logan," he repeated.

Logan raised his hand in the air to acknowledge his brother's concern as he went out the back door.

But he honestly did have every intention of being cautious. Not only about the case and Harry Denton, but about Maddie. About his feelings for her and what was happening between them.

It was just that caution didn't seem to be slowing things down any.

MADDIE WAS PACING the front porch when Logan arrived. She hadn't been able to just sit still and wait for him. Not since the mail had come and Bernice had brought her the envelope marked, To Be Opened by Madeline Van Waltonscot Only.

The letter—note, really—hadn't been delivered yet when Maddie had called Logan that morning to tell him Bernice had arranged a two o'clock appointment for them with Madeline Van Waltonscot's lawyer, and a three o'clock meeting with the accountant for the following day because he was out of town until then.

As Maddie had hung up, the personal assistant had brought in the envelope and, having read what was inside, Maddie had been pacing ever since. First in her rooms until even that large space had begun to seem claustrophobic, then downstairs until the staff had started to look worried that she might be on the verge of exploding, and finally out on the porch where she could keep an eye out for Logan.

She was grateful that he was punctual, pulling up the driveway at exactly one-thirty. The moment she set eyes on him she felt better. Not good, but better.

"Maddie?" he said as he got out of the red Jeep, apparently seeing that she was upset and forgoing any other greeting because of it.

"Hi," she answered feebly as he climbed the six steps to the porch.

He had on charcoal slacks and a dove gray dress shirt, and both worked to bring out the heather color of his gorgeous eyes. She had the unholy urge to walk into his arms, kiss him hello and start up today where they'd left off the night before.

But of course she didn't do that.

Instead, when he was near enough she held out the note. "This came in the mail a little while ago."

He removed the plain white sheet of typing paper from the equally plain envelope and read the typed words out loud. " 'I made an anonymous call to the wife's employer. She was fired the next day. Have contacted cooperative official to revoke husband's license. Will give him the option of leaving the state first.' "

Maddie cringed.

Logan looked it over, back and front, then did the same with the envelope. "No signature, no return address. Just a Denver postmark."

"Denver, not Thornton, where Harry Denton is. Maybe we're barking up the wrong tree with him," she said with concern echoing in her voice.

"He had a ton of parking tickets in Denver, so apparently he spends a lot of time in the city. He could easily have mailed this while he was there, so that doesn't necessarily mean anything."

"I hope you're right. It's so horrible that people are having these awful things done to them at someone else's request. Someone else who I am now."

Just thinking about it made her too agitated to stand still. She started to pace again, wringing her hands together as she went on more to herself than to Logan.

"Getting somebody fired. Having a license revoked that probably allows a person to work. Whoever these people are, they're having their lives torn up. And if I was sent back here to fix things, why wasn't I given some sort of help? Why was it done in a way that leaves me in the dark while more bad things go on happening?"

Logan caught her by the arms. "Hey. We're working on finding out what's going on so we can put an end to it."

"But how much damage will be done by the time we do?"

"No matter how much is done, we'll make it right."

That he spoke with such confidence and included himself in the solution helped her more than he could ever know. "Do you mean that? You'll help me fix whatever is wrong? You won't just figure it all out and then disappear on me?"

"What do you think I'm going to do? Dump it in your lap and take off? I'm in for the distance, here, lady. I'll see it through to the end."

Then what? a voice in the back of her mind asked. But she pushed it away. Finding out what was going on and stopping it, repairing the damage that had been done—those were the things that were important.

"Thank you," she said, trying to force a more businesslike tone into her voice. And failing.

"Just doing my job, ma'am," he joked, but something in his expression, in the way he rubbed her arms in a slow, sensual massage, told her his kidding was only a cover-up for the much more complicated struggle that was going on in him, too, over what was happening between them.

"We'll set things straight. Don't worry about it," he told her.

She nodded, not only letting herself be bolstered by him physically, mentally and emotionally, but giving in to trusting that everything would work out, too. "You're a nice man, do you know that?" she said, managing a small smile.

"I know. I'm a prince of a guy," he joked again, bathing her in a perfect grin of his own.

"I don't know if I'd go that far. An earl or a duke, maybe," she countered.

He let go of her, refolded the note, put it back in the envelope and handed it to her. "Come on. Keep that in your purse for now and we'll put it with the others later. If we don't get going we'll miss this appointment with the lawyer."

"And we can't do that. The sooner we get this thing solved, the better," she agreed, all the while regretting that she didn't have his hands on her anymore.

She took the envelope to the whitewashed railing that ran around the porch's edge, where she'd left her purse and the navy blue jacket that matched her slacks.

Logan was right behind her to help her put the jacket on over the tapestry vest and snowy white, high-collared blouse she wore. But once it was in place she again lost his touch. Then she got it back when she turned to go down the stairs because he took her elbow along the way to help her into the Jeep.

Maybe she'd gone crazy, she thought, to be so intensely aware of such minor contact, such simple courtesies. But, crazy or not, she just couldn't help herself.

"So. I know we're on a mission to get a copy of whatever wills are in effect, but what else are we fishing for today?" she asked in an effort to distract her wayward thoughts.

Before she knew it they were at the downtown Denver offices of Burns, Burns & Burns.

The law firm occupied two of four row houses that had been completely renovated on the east edge of the city. Salvaged from the jaws of decay, they were now restored to their original dignity on the outside and commanded rents no mere mortals could afford.

Burns, Burns & Burns apparently had no problem with that.

Inside the three-story brownstone was an elegant reception area that combined cool, calming pastels and modern art in the wall sculptures that all looked like wind-washed sand dunes tipped with pale whispers of lavender, mauve and lime green.

Maddie had only to approach the receptionist's island and draw one glance before the young woman jumped to her feet. "Miss Van Waltonscot! So nice to see you! Mr. Burns said to bring you back the minute you arrived. Can I get you a cup of espresso? Or a soda? Or Tea? Or—"

"We're fine, thanks," Maddie answered to stop the gush, trying a smile to put the woman at ease.

"Please, come right this way."

The receptionist led them down a hall to the first door on the left, knocked once and opened an oak door labeled Melvin Burns.

A man of about sixty with white hair and large, protruding ears was already pushing away from the glass table that served as his desk. He hurried to Maddie, grasping her hand in both of his when he reached her.

"My dear! How good it is to see you looking so well!" he gushed, too. Maybe it was office policy.

"Thank you," Maddie answered. "And thank you—the firm—for the flowers that were sent to the hospital when I woke up. They were really pretty."

His mouth kept on smiling, but his bushy eyebrows dipped together in a split-second frown.

Maddie realized belatedly that she probably should have said the flowers were 'lovely', or something more in keeping with the way Madeline Van Waltonscot would have phrased it. But it was too late now so she didn't try amending her words. Instead she introduced Logan, who had drawn a questioning glance from the attorney.

"We use Strummel Investigations, but I don't recall hearing your name," he said with faint attempt to cover his suspicion.

"I've only recently joined the agency."

"I see," the older man said, ushering Maddie to a chair in front of his desk as if he were claiming ownership of her and putting distance between her and Logan. "Well, why don't you go out and tell our receptionist who you are, ask her to introduce you around so everyone will be apprised of Strummel Investigations' newest member? Then perhaps you have something else to do while Miss Van Waltonscot and I talk.''

The lawyer's tone was one he might have used to dismiss an errand boy—patronizing, condescending. He even spoke more slowly, as if Logan were dim-witted.

Understandably, Logan didn't like the treatment. Maddie saw it in the tightening of his features, the thin, hard smile on his lips. ''Logan will need to be in on this meeting,'' she decreed, surprising herself with how firm she sounded. ''He's here to help me.''

''Help you?'' the attorney repeated dubiously, looking Logan over from head to toe. ''Yes, well, I'm sure he can be very helpful with other things, but you might want to reconsider having him in here, my dear. After all, what we discuss is confidential.''

''He needs to be here,'' she said even more forcefully.

The lawyer looked from Maddie to Logan and back again, obviously unhappy with the situation, and Logan personally.

But not as unhappy as Maddie was with him for insulting Logan. It seemed that the old Madeline Van Waltonscot was not alone in her arrogance and sense of superiority.

Finally the attorney inclined his head, accepting the situation, however reluctantly. He urged Maddie to sit in one of the leather-and-chrome chairs to which he'd guided her while Logan took the second. The older man seemed intent on ignoring him.

''I certainly hope it isn't a problem that's brought you into the office,'' he said as he headed for his own chair behind the glass table again. "You know I'm always happy to come to the house to discuss whatever is on your mind."

Oh, great, Maddie thought, *another slip out of character.* "We were going to be around here today, anyway," she lied to explain it. Then, before he could say anything else, she went on. "Let me get right to the point so we don't take too much of your time—"

Another of those smiling frowns. "My dear, I'm at your disposal for the entire afternoon. I've cleared my calendar for you."

"You shouldn't have done that. This won't take long. I didn't mean for you to cancel other people just for me."

The frown lingered and the smile froze, and she knew she was getting herself in deeper and deeper. Clearly she was sitting across from yet another person who knew the real Madeline Van Waltonscot well. Certainly well enough to know she'd have thought nothing of a high-powered attorney casting off an entire half day of other clients for her on the spur of the moment.

She sat up straighter and used a more formal tone to get down to business so she could finish with this as soon as possible. "I'm afraid the accident has left me with some gaps in my memory. I was hoping you might be able to fill them for me. And I'd also like a copy of all the wills—past and present—that apply to the Van Waltonscot estate."

"*All* the wills? But there's only the one left by your father when he passed on. You know your mother didn't have one when she died the year before. She didn't need one—nothing was in her name. And as for anything current, I've been trying to persuade you to allow me to draw one up. Actually, I was hoping that after the close call of the accident..." His voice trailed off as if he'd ventured into a delicate topic.

"As Miss Van Waltonscot said," Logan put in, "she has some gaps in her memory. You'll have to forgive her for anything she's no longer aware of."

The lawyer acknowledged Logan by sliding his gaze in Logan's direction without moving his head. "Am I to assume you, too, are helping to 'fill the gaps'?"

"I'm trying to help her discover what she's forgotten, yes," Logan answered in measured tones.

An ugly little smile skittered across the attorney's mouth, but he pushed a button on a desk intercom and asked someone to make a copy of the Van Waltonscot will.

When that was done Maddie continued. "I have a vague recollection of getting you to recommend a private investigator but, odd as it may seem, I don't remember what I wanted one for before. Did I mention my initial reason to you?"

Melvin Burns seemed to ignore Logan again. "I wish I could be of some assistance, but I don't know why you wanted the name of a detective. You didn't say. In fact, you were very clear about not wanting to discuss it with me."

Clear enough to have offended him, if the indignation underlying his tone was any indication.

"Did you also recommend a man named Harry Denton, by any chance?" Logan asked.

The lawyer addressed Maddie as if she'd been the one to pose the question. "Harry Denton? No, I don't know who that is." And he didn't much care. Instead he showed his suspicions once more. "I'd been led to understand that you had returned to perfect health since the accident. No one said anything about memory loss."

"It's only gaps here and there," Maddie assured him. "And I should also warn you that there's been a change in my motor skills—for instance, my handwriting is different now, so you'll find my signature is not the same. I'm told a head injury can produce both effects. But since that's all I was left with and I'm otherwise shipshape, I consider it a blessing."

"Shipshape" seemed to have been another misstep because the lawyer stared at her for a moment before he said, "The head injury seems to have altered more than your memory and motor functions. I've never known you to be so... Well, it's almost as if you have a new lease on life," he finished, seeming to opt for the best way he could think to put it.

"I do, actually," Maddie agreed. "Coming that near to death has altered the way I think, the way I look at things and people, at everything, really. So I guess I'm not the woman I used to be." In fact, she was getting pretty brave to make a remark like that.

"Well, we're all just glad you're back with us after such a horrible ordeal. And looking even better than—"

Two knocks on the door interrupted him as a very young man in a too-tight shirt collar came in carrying a manila envelope. He handed it to Melvin Burns, muttered something and left.

The lawyer looked inside and then gave it to Maddie. "That's the will. Can I persuade you to do some preliminaries on one of your own now?"

"Maybe later. Today we have some other things to do and can't stay."

Maddie stood, and Logan and the attorney followed suit.

She didn't know whether or not to extend her hand to the attorney but ended up doing it, pulling it back some and then shoving it at the older man again.

He clasped it between both of his the same way he had when she'd first come in, holding it as he rounded his desk and led her to the door. "I know you've endured a nightmare in that accident, but I'm glad that you've come through it so well. In fact, you seem even more energetic than you were before. All that tension that had settled in is gone. You're so much more calm and relaxed and . . . happy. Perhaps it's better if some of the gaps in your memory aren't filled and whatever had troubled you stays in the past," he finished with a sidelong glare at Logan.

"Oh, I don't think I could let things lay," she said.

The attorney walked them all the way to the front entrance of the building as if he were a doorman. "If there's anything else I can do for you, any other questions I can answer, don't hesitate to call."

"I won't."

"And let's get together on that new will soon."

"Sure."

Only when the lawyer was certain Maddie was finished with him did he turn back into the office, looking through Logan and not so much as saying goodbye to him, as if he would no longer recognize his presence.

"I'm sorry!" Maddie said when the door closed behind him. "I guess Madeline Van Waltonscot isn't the only one under the impression that she's better than other people."

Logan shrugged. "It wasn't your fault, and it was no big deal. Forget it."

That wasn't easy to do, but Maddie was at a loss as to what to say beyond the apology.

They'd reached the Jeep by then and Logan helped her into it. Then he went around to the driver's side and got in himself.

"I'm really glad that's over," she confided. "I felt like a bad imposter who was going to be found out any minute."

"You did fine." He nodded toward the envelope in her lap. "Why don't you read the will to us on the way out to Thornton?"

Maddie settled back, removed the sheets of paper from the envelope and began to read the document.

It took the whole drive to the northeast suburb to get through it all, even though it was pretty straightforward once she'd cut through the legalese.

Eight years ago, at the death of her father, Madeline Van Waltonscot had inherited everything he'd owned. Grocery stores, stocks, bonds, houses, cars, a meat-packing plant, a cannery, a whole fleet of trucks, a yacht, a vast collection of art and other cash and personal assets that had amounted to a staggering fortune.

No one else was mentioned in the will, nor were there any stipulations or conditions ruling it. The Van Waltonscot estate was all—free and clear—Madeline Van Waltonscot's, to do with as she pleased.

The document didn't have any clues that would help Maddie and Logan discover who the husband and wife were in the anonymous notes, any reason anyone would be bothering the heiress or why it would require hiring someone to wreak havoc in their lives to get them to stop.

But under the shock of learning the extent of the fortune, Maddie could hardly think about what they hadn't learned. Instead, when Logan finally located the other detective's residence, her head was still spinning. Dazed, she followed him across the weed-ridden, overgrown yard to the run-down, ramshackle house.

Not that he required anything of her. No one was there and he was perfectly capable of peeking in the windows himself, pointing out an answering machine in pieces, as if Harry Denton had tried to play repair-man—which accounted for not even a machine answering their calls to the place.

In the end, Logan left a note in Harry Denton's mailbox, informing him to call Madeline Van Waltonscot immediately.

Only when they got back in the Jeep and Maddie had stuffed the envelope with the will in her purse to get it out of her sight, did she regain her wits.

Or maybe it had more to do with the fact that once again the day was drawing to a close, they were headed back to the estate and she was likely on the verge of losing Logan's company.

"Are you busy tonight?" she asked when she'd snapped out of her stupor.

"No, I'm free. Why?"

"I was just wondering if I could bribe you with a dinner of divine hot dogs to help me out with something." Oh, how fast the wheels of her mind could turn when the threat of his leaving was in the air!

"Must not be too important if the bribe only involves hot dogs."

"Okay, so I have a double motive. I'm dying for a hot dog *and* I need your help."

"Doing what?"

"Taking down that huge painting that faces my bed. The eye staring out of that triangle is giving me the creeps. But when I asked Bernice if we could see about having a couple of the housemen move it, she got all horrified about entrusting such a thing to them and I backed down."

"It's an original Picasso, Maddie."

"I know. But that eye..." She grimaced. "You just don't know what it's like to wake up in the middle of the night, with the moonlight falling on it, and have it looking at me. It isn't as if I'm going to hurt the painting. I only want to put it somewhere else. But it's so big it requires two people to move it. Besides, there's hot dogs in payment," she enticed as if she were offering solid gold. "We'll blow the last of my— Maggie Morgan's—money. I had an emergency twenty-dollar bill stashed in the purse that you got back from Designs Unlimited. That'll buy us some pretty good hot dogs."

"And I'll bet you know just the place for it."

"A place called Mustard's Last Stand. Are you game?"

He glanced at her from the corner of his eye as if she were out of her mind. But only for a moment before breaking into a grin. "I'm in."

They indulged in cheese fries and hot dogs slathered in chili and spicy mustard and split a slice of cheesecake for dessert—but only after vowing to walk it off once they'd moved the painting.

Then they went back to the Van Waltonscot estate, informed the maid who let them in that the house staff could feast on whatever delicacies the chef had prepared for dinner and went upstairs to Maddie's room.

"Now be honest," she said as they stood before the painting that took up nearly a full wall. "Would you like to have that watching you sleep?"

The painting was a cubist portrait of a woman with a single eye that bored down from the canvas with an unrelenting glare.

"A bedroom doesn't seem like the best spot for it, no," Logan agreed. "Besides, I'd think any steam coming from the bathroom would be bad for it."

"Good point! I'll use it as my excuse when I have to explain why I went ahead and took it down. Now let's get it out of here."

Logan pulled the chair from the dressing table and a tufted one from the corner of the room, then situated them on either side of the artwork so they could both get up near the top, where it was bracketed securely to the wall.

It required some finagling to get it free, but they finally managed, lowering the frame to the floor before they could step down.

"Where to?" Logan asked.

"The TV room, I think. Oh, excuse me—I mean the sitting room. I raise eyebrows when I call it the TV room."

They again hoisted it on either side and carefully moved the piece to its destination, turning it face first toward the wall to protect the painting.

That was when Maddie spotted the small book the size of a paperback stuck in the corner of the frame on Logan's side.

"What's that?"

He bent over and retrieved it as Maddie joined him.

"Looks like an old ledger."

Maddie leaned over Logan's arm to see for herself as he turned the pages, studying what was written on each one.

"It's definitely a woman's handwriting but not anything like Madeline Van Waltonscot's from the day planner. This is so tiny and florid it's almost more like someone drew the letters and numbers instead of writing them. And there are monthly entries that ended—" he paused until he found the last one "—nine years ago."

Something about that time period rang a bell, but at first Maddie couldn't figure out what it was. Then it occurred to her. "The lawyer said Madeline Van Waltonscot's father died eight years ago—a year *after* her mother."

"Hmm. That's an interesting coincidence." He went on studying the ledger. "As interesting as the fact that every entry is meticulously dated, but there's no stipulation as to who or what received the money."

"Do you think this belonged to Madeline Van Waltonscot's mother and she had a lover she was paying?" Maddie asked with a note of delicious scandal in her voice.

"I don't know. The amounts are small enough that she could probably have taken the money out of some sort of allowance without causing any suspicion. But—" He stopped short as he discovered a photograph in the back of the leather-bound book.

It was a graduation picture of a young man who bore such a striking resemblance to Maddie that they could have been fraternal twins. And on the back, in that same flowery script, was written, Steven, High School Graduation, 1974.

"Another Van Waltonscot child?" Maddie whispered.

Logan did some mathematical calculations out loud and then said, "That would make him four years older, and with the resemblance, I'd say this guy being Madeline Van Waltonscot's brother is pretty likely."

It took Maddie a moment to assimilate the news. Then questions began popping into her mind so fast it made her dizzy.

"I think I need that walk now. And the fresh air that goes with it to think about this."

Logan nodded and handed her the ledger. "Keep it with the day planner and we'll take it with us to the accountant tomorrow to see if he knows anything about it."

The day planner was back in the bedroom, and Logan trailed her there as she did as she was told. Then, without saying anything else, they went downstairs, out the front door and headed along a path, which, Maddie knew from exploring the grounds, wound through a maze of sculptured bushes and gardens full of mums.

"A brother," she murmured shortly after they'd left the house. "Had you ever heard there was another Van Waltonscot?"

"No, but it isn't as if I've been an avid follower of the family tree."

"Do you suppose he wasn't a Van Waltonscot? That he was the mother's illegitimate son or something?"

"Anything is possible, but the resemblance to you is so striking that I find it hard to believe you didn't have both of the same parents."

"That's true. But if he was legitimate, why would the mother have given him money on the sly? Or at least what seems like on the sly?"

"Maybe she wasn't giving it to him, Maybe she was stashing it somewhere to buy him something."

"For years and years?"

Logan just shrugged. "Or maybe the picture being in the ledger is only a coincidence. Maybe one thing doesn't have anything to do with the other."

"That seems less likely than the lover theory. But why wasn't this Steven mentioned in the will if he was another child?" Maddie asked.

"He could be dead. Maybe he died shortly after the mother but before the father. If that was the case, there wouldn't be any reason for him to be in the will."

"Or maybe he's the voice on the answering machine. Maybe he's who's bothering Madeline Van Waltonscot and who she wanted discouraged."

"If he's alive, then he'd probably feel entitled to a share of this estate," Logan agreed, referring to the splendor through which they walked and going on to remind her about the reason Madeline Van Waltonscot had tried to hire Quinn in the first place.

"But wouldn't he just contest the will through legal channels instead of bothering her for it?" she asked, glancing up at Logan's handsome profile bathed in moonlight.

He shrugged. "Who knows? As I said before, when there's money involved it's hard to figure what people will do. To get it or to keep it."

They walked in silence with the back of the house in view as they rounded it and headed toward the front on the opposite side from which they'd begun.

"You realize, though, that we could be barking up the wrong tree altogether," Logan said then. "From the sound of those messages on the answering machine, the caller is not the aggressor. Madeline Van Waltonscot—or Harry Denton on her behalf—is."

"Meaning the ledger doesn't have any bearing at all. It's just something we happened to find tonight," Maddie summarized. "Okay, but since we're talking about the man on the answering machine and him not being the aggressor, why would Madeline Van Waltonscot be the one going after him and his wife no matter who he is?"

"How about an affair of the heart instead of an affair of the purse strings?"

"An affair?"

"Maybe Madeline Van Waltonscot and the man on the answering machine were involved, he ended it to stay with his wife and Harry Denton's been hired to mete out retribution. You know what they say about hell having no fury like a woman scorned."

"It's a possibility, I suppose," Maddie conceded halfheartedly. "But then the heiress would be the one who was doing the bothering, not the other way around, the way she told your brother."

"Except that that could have just been intended to make what she wanted him to do sound good. An excuse to get a P.I. to do the dirty work that's really just her revenge."

"I don't know," Maddie admitted. "But if I had to guess, I'd say the guy on the answering machine is Steven and that he was trying to get his half of the estate."

"That does seem the most likely."

They'd reached the front of the house, and as they climbed the steps to the porch Maddie said, "Still, though, with all there is, why wouldn't Madeline Van Waltonscot just share?" She leaned her back against one of the pillars that supported the veranda on the second and third floors.

Logan stopped directly in front of her, smiling down at her. "Maddie. You knew Madeline Van Walton-scot. Did she seem like the kind of person who would do that if she didn't have to? Or did she seem like the kind of person who would hoard all the marbles and get a bully to keep her from having to give up any of them?"

The sight of Logan's perfect masculine face set off sparks in her stomach, so Maddie stared at his broad chest instead. "You're right. The person I knew would have been stingy." Maddie took a deep breath and sighed it out forlornly. "Oh, boy. The more I find out about her, the less I like her. And now I have to live in her skin for the rest of my life. This bitchy, selfish snob. Yuk."

Logan reached a hand to the pole above her head and bent to her ear. "You may have to live in her skin, but you aren't the same woman," he said in a consoling gust of wickedly warm air. Then he pushed himself away from her, but not so far as to remove his hand from above her or leave more than a few inches between them.

"Still," she said, "I get the blame for what she did and what she was."

He kissed the tip of her nose. "It'll turn around." Another kiss, this time on the chin.

"I don't know. There seems to be more and more to fix."

"You're up for the job."

She was up for something, all right, but it didn't seem to be work. It had more to do with those small kisses he was teasing her with. And the rain of delight they were sending all through her.

She answered it by kissing his chin when it came within her reach. "I think it would have been a lot easier to have just won the lottery," she mused on her way to nuzzling his Adam's apple when he kissed her ear.

"True," he agreed. "But then we wouldn't have had any reason to meet."

"Ah, back to the grand-design theory," she said just before he completely captured her mouth with his.

The kiss began as playfully as the others had been, but it didn't take long for it to turn to something more. Something much more.

His lips parted, his tongue formed a bridge and Maddie found herself pulled away from the pillar and pressed to the hard wall of his body.

That rain of delight he'd started in her moments earlier turned to a torrential downpour that wiped away all thoughts except the pleasure of it. Maddie slipped her arms around him, splaying her hands over the honed muscles of his back, reveling in the feel of him as he deepened the kiss even more.

Lord, but the man could kiss!

And tonight he showed her just how well. How perfectly. How passionately.

His tongue circled hers, plundered, thrust in and out in a dance too much like making love not to leave vivid images of just that in her mind.

His hands were suddenly in her hair, holding her to him as he taught her how much he could arouse with just his mouth over hers.

Then his kisses trailed across her cheek, behind her earlobe, along the line of her jaw as his hands eased her head backward to free her throat to his seeking tongue.

The cool night air bathed the heated skin of her face, and Maddie's eyes drifted open just slightly.

But it was enough.

Enough to see the huge house looming all around them. Enough to remind her that it was full of people, of expectations, of complications . . .

"We're doing it again," she breathed in a lament, regretting the words that stopped Logan even as she said them.

He laughed a little wryly, pushed her head downward and dropped his brow to the top of it. "You're right. We are. I only started this to lighten things up so you wouldn't feel bad, but it seems like that's all it takes for us to get carried away, doesn't it?"

"Mmm." But she definitely didn't feel bad anymore. At least not the way she had before.

He let go of her, stepped away and pointed a long thick finger at her as he gave orders. "Go inside. Lock the door. And I'll see you tomorrow."

She nodded, wanting badly to grab his hand and pull him with her.

But she knew better. Knew that the last thing she needed now was to get in any deeper with Logan when she was already in over her head in other things.

"Good night," she answered him, going into the house.

"Night," he said, watching her as if he meant to stay on that porch until she closed the door the way he'd told her to.

But she didn't do it.

She knew she was courting danger, but she just stood there, in silent invitation for him to come in, too. To continue what they'd begun.

And then he crossed the porch, and she thought that was what he was going to do.

But instead he reached in and pulled the door closed himself. As if only then could he actually leave her.

Maddie heard his retreating steps on the painted wood floor outside, down the stairs. She heard him open the Jeep door and then close it, too. But he didn't start the engine for a long, long time.

And even when he finally did and drove away, she knew he'd been wanting her as much as she wanted him, that he'd been torn between staying and going.

She just didn't know how anything could possibly be done about it while so many other things hung over her head.

Chapter Six

"I don't like it."

"I know, you told me that when I called you this morning. But it's the only way he would agree to meet me." Maddie was once again riding in the passenger seat of Logan's Jeep, on their way to the accountant's office the next day.

But it wasn't the accountant they were talking about.

"Harry Denton is a sleazebag with a record a mile long in California, who lost his investigator's license there and came here, no doubt because he didn't have to be licensed at all. Calling himself a P.I. is only putting a nice title on the fact that he's a hood for hire. And we're meeting him in an abandoned warehouse on Wasser Street at the height of rush hour, when traffic bogs everything down and getting a cop there if things go sour will be next to impossible."

"He wouldn't answer any questions on the phone and didn't want to meet me at all. He said I'd set the rules—no contact under any circumstances, updates only through the anonymous notes. He became very suspicious when I told him I needed to ask him a few questions and to talk about what it is he's doing."

"Let me guess—he figured you'd suddenly gotten cold feet over what he's done so far and wanted to back out of whatever deal you made with him, before he's scared whoever he's scaring enough to get them out of the way, and consequently also from causing him any problems."

Maddie glanced at Logan, enjoying the sight of his chiseled profile, of him dressed in jeans, a crisp yellow shirt and a corduroy blazer, if not enjoying the conversation and the fact that he was less than happy with her. "I'll bet you were a good cop," she answered, because his guess was right on the money.

"Do you know how dangerous this is, Maddie?" he countered.

"It was the only way," she repeated.

Logan shook his head slowly. "I better drop you off somewhere after this appointment with the accountant and go alone."

"You can't do that. He told me to come by myself. If you're there and I'm not he definitely won't answer any questions. He's not going to like you being there at all. I can guarantee that."

"Damn it."

Maddie thought it a propitious time to change the subject. "What did you find out about Steven?" she asked, knowing Logan had spent the earlier part of the day doing a computer check and going to the records department to search for something that might lead them to the Steven in the picture they'd found with the ledger.

Logan gave her a stern sideways glance that let her know he might allow the subject change but it didn't mean he was any happier with the arrangements she'd made to meet Harry Denton when he'd finally called just before noon.

"There wasn't a Steven Van Waltonscot in the phone book. Not under that name, not under Waltonscot or Walton or Scott. I did find a birth certificate for a Steven Van Waltonscot, born August 10, 1956, to Horace and Selina Van Waltonscot, so he is— or was—Madeline Van Waltonscot's brother, all right. But there's also no driver's license, no record of military service of any kind, no marriage certificate, no police record—"

"So he must have died, too."

"Except that there's no death certificate, either."

"Could he have moved to a different state?"

"There's also no Social Security number or credit report—both of which would show up no matter where he lives."

"He exists but he doesn't exist."

"Sort of. He doesn't exist as Steven Van Waltonscot."

"Meaning?"

"He's either living under a different name or died under one."

"Ah . . . But how do we find him if we don't know what name he's using?"

"Not easily. What we do is ask around and try to come up with someone who knows what name he might use, or has any idea where he is, what he does for a living, things like that."

"Or maybe Harry Denton will just tell us everything about whom he's harassing and why and where we can contact them to make amends," she said on an upbeat note.

Logan parked in front of the small redbrick office building of the accountant, Josiah Franklin, turned off the engine and looked her in the eye. "You really think he's going to be that forthcoming, Pollyanna?"

She shrugged and pulled a face. "We can hope, can't we?"

Logan just laughed wryly and got out of the Jeep.

But as he did his blazer came open just enough for Maddie to catch a glimpse of a shoulder holster.

"You brought a gun?" she whispered when she'd hurried out of the passenger side and met him on the sidewalk.

"Did you think I was going to take you to meet a thug in a deserted warehouse and not bring my gun?"

Suddenly what Maddie had been considering an adventure took on a more serious overtone.

Then the office door opened and a very elderly gentleman greeted Maddie with the genuine fondness of a kindly uncle.

"Madeline, Madeline, it's so good to see you up and about and well!" he said as he ushered them inside, past several cubicles where other men and women worked and into an inner conference room where a tray with several serviceable mugs, a coffee carafe, cream, sugar and a plate of what looked to be home-made cookies awaited them.

Maddie introduced Logan and used the same explanation for his presence that she'd used with the lawyer as she and Logan settled into comfortable but unimpressive vinyl chairs with coffee and cookies.

The accountant took the news of her swiss-cheese memory with less suspicion than the lawyer had. He relayed his sympathy and was eager to be convinced her only other ill effect was the alteration in her motor skills. But he kept shooting disapproving glances Logan's way, and as both Maddie and Logan plied him with questions, he was clearly less at ease answering Logan's than Maddie's.

They tried to establish if Josiah Franklin had been aware of anything unusual going on with her finances before the accident—if she'd gone through a greater than normal amount of money, or had instructed him to pay anyone out of the ordinary, or anyone named Harry Denton specifically.

The silver-haired octogenarian assured Maddie that nothing strange had been going on at all that he had any knowledge of and that he'd never heard the name Harry Denton.

Then he turned the tables to inquire pointedly if Logan were charging her a fee for his services.

"Of course he's charging me," Maddie said before Logan could answer for himself. "I went to him, asked for his help and hired him."

Something about that made Logan chuckle even as he tried to hide it behind a cough.

Maddie ignored both that and the elderly man's cleared throat and got back to the subject at hand. "We found this hidden behind a painting," she said, handing him the ledger. "Would you know anything about it?"

He opened it, extending his arm to better see it even with the aid of thick glasses that made his eyes seem unnaturally large, and went through the first few pages. "I don't recognize the ledger or the account from which the money was withdrawn. In fact, this particular bank hasn't been in existence for many years—it merged with two others. But the handwriting is your mother's—or did you know that?"

"I thought it was."

"But without a name or names to establish who the money was paid to, I'm afraid I couldn't begin to tell you anything about it."

Maddie handed him the graduation photograph. "This was in the back of it."

Bushy white eyebrows rose above the frames of the glasses. "Ah, of course. Your brother. She must have been giving him money behind your father's back."

But the words came out harshly, and the moment they were spoken Josiah Franklin seemed to regret having said them. He gave the ledger and the picture back to Maddie as if he wanted nothing more to do with them. "Now we'd better deal with this change in your signature."

"Before we get into that, we'd like to know more about Steven, if we could," Logan interrupted. "He seems to be a particular blank in Maddie's—Miss Van Waltonscot's—memory, and we have reason to believe he may have tried to contact her."

The old man drew himself up in the chair he occupied across the table and fixed Logan with an icy glare. "I won't discuss Steven Van Waltonscot."

"But I just want to know where he is, if he's well, how I can reach him," Maddie said.

"I wouldn't know any of that, nor do I care to. I was your grandfather's best friend from the time we were boys. I always thought of your father as one of my sons and you as one of my grandchildren. But Steven was a different matter entirely. He turned bad and your family was better off without him."

"My mother must not have felt that way if she gave him money behind my father's back."

Josiah Franklin shook his head again. "A mother is the last person to see a child's true colors. And even when she does, she loves that child in spite of them. Now," he said with loud finality, "to the business of your signature."

Maddie glanced at Logan, but the almost infinitesimal shrug he gave her let her know there was no way of getting the old man to talk. Instead he nodded toward the accountant and Maddie turned her attention to what he was saying.

"I wondered why I hadn't been receiving notices on your accounts due around town. I know you must have been weak and not in the mood for shopping, but I expected at least a bill for a gown to wear to the Unessa Ball. A mere two nights away and you without a dress?" he finished with a return to his friendly role, as if the subject of Steven Van Waltonscot had never been broached.

"The Unessa Ball," Maddie repeated. "Oh, yes, I recall something coming in the mail about it but there's been so much on my mind, I didn't pay a lot of attention to it. I don't think I'll be going, anyway."

"Not going? Of course you have to go. You're on the board of the foundation that it benefits. We've all understood that you were in no condition to help arrange for the fund-raiser this year, but surely you're well enough to attend. Your family started the foundation—there's never been a year that the Van Waltonscots weren't present."

"Yes, but—"

"I think it would be a good idea," Logan said in a way that left no doubt, in Maddie's mind at least, that he had an ulterior motive.

"Of course it's a good idea," the elderly man snapped, as if Logan were an upstart whose support he didn't need or want. "Everyone is anxious to see you and wish you their best. It's the perfect opportunity to get back into the swing of things."

Clearly she didn't have any option. "Sure. I guess we'll go," she conceded, unable to even feign any enthusiasm.

"We? Will Mr. Strummel be your escort?"

"Yes. If I have to go, he has to go," she said, aiming the answer as much at Logan as at the elderly man.

"I see. Well, so long as you attend, I suppose that's all that's important." Then he once again got back to business. "This is what we'll do about the change in signature. I'll just have you sign your full name to this." He passed her a plain sheet of paper.

While Maddie wrote Madeline Van Waltonscot, he said, "I'll notarize it and then have it faxed immediately to every account and bank that requires your signature, along with a letter explaining what's happened. You can go right out and shop for a gown without any problem whatsoever." He did the notarizing as he finished the explanation. "And then we'll be seeing you at the ball."

There wasn't any more to say about that or about anything else they'd come to the accountant for, so Maddie took the initiative and stood.

The elderly man walked them out, again telling her how happy he was that she was fully recovered and inviting her to have dinner with him and his family soon. But, like the lawyer the day before, no goodbyes were said to Logan.

Still, when he and Maddie were back in the Jeep, she had more than that slight on her mind. "I know you must have a good reason for it, but I really don't want to go to some high-society function where I'll feel like a fish out of water.''

''I did have a good reason for it. Remember what I said about our needing to ask around, to try finding someone who knows something about Steven Van Waltonscot? Well, the circle in which Madeline Van Waltonscot travels is tight and has been for generations. A few casual questions about the heiress's family—using our gaps-in-the-memory story—might get us an answer or two we could use as a lead.''

''Aha!'' Maddie said as if he'd just opened her eyes. ''And in the process we might find someone willing to tell us whatever it was that Josiah Franklin didn't want to talk about.''

''Exactly.''

''And you'll go with me?'' she asked.

That made him hesitate, and before he could answer, Maddie went on. ''I know. This guy was another one like the lawyer with his nose in the air and this ball thing will probably be full of them. I don't know where they get off acting like that. And then there was that laugh under your breath from you. What was that all about?''

Logan glanced at her from the corner of his eye. ''I had the feeling this guy thought I'd been hired for services other than investigating. It's something I've heard Madeline Van Waltonscot had a tendency to do. One of the cops who worked security regularly claimed she propositioned him more than once. The story was that she promised to put him on the payroll as her bodyguard, except what she wanted him to do to her body was more than guard it.''

Maddie grimaced. "He thought you were my boy toy?"

Logan laughed wryly. "That's one way of putting it."

"Oh, yuck. I was thinking he and the lawyer were just horrible snobs, but that's even worse."

"They're snobs, all right. That's part of it. A P.I. is certainly not in the same league as an heiress and her highbrow legal firm or business manager."

"And on top of it, there you are," Maddie added, "looking like Mr. July on the hunk-of-the-month calendar, and their dirty minds kicked in. I don't like it."

"Thrills the hell out of me, too, I can tell you."

"So you're not any happier about going to this ball thing than I am."

"No. But we need to do it."

Maddie took a deep breath and sighed it out. "Okay. But I'm going on record that I'd rather spend the evening in my blue jeans, in some nice cozy place like my old house, sitting on the floor eating pizza and watching television, and if nothing comes of this I'm going to exact revenge on you."

"Worse revenge than my having to go as your boy toy?"

"Much."

"I'm shaking in my boots."

"You should be."

He glanced at the clock on the dashboard. "Now let's do some preparation for this little rendezvous you've arranged for us and hope it doesn't exact its own revenge."

THERE WERE ALLEYS along both sides of the warehouse on Wasser Street and train tracks that ran be-

hind a loading dock in back. Maddie and Logan
arrived at the meeting place earlier than scheduled so
Logan could have a look around. When he had, they
stepped over a homeless man who seemed to be passed
out in the doorway of the building.

The door had once had a full-pane window center,
but now the glass was broken out, and of the boards
that had been nailed across it, only one remained—
high enough up to duck under and go in.

Logan led the way, but even so, Maddie heard the
scurry of mice—rats, maybe—when she followed.

She tried not to think about it.

Or about spiders or cockroaches or anything else
that might inhabit the place.

What they entered was a small room mostly taken
up by what had no doubt been a sales counter once
upon a time. But nothing had been sold there for dec-
ades, and dust and cobwebs were the only things cur-
rently in stock.

They rounded the counter. Before Logan went
through the door behind it, he pushed the scarred
panel open and peered cautiously inside.

Light fell from holes in the roof and from one
loading-dock bay at the opposite end, but still the
place was full of shadows. More sounds Maddie didn't
want to attribute greeted them before silence followed
their steps into the actual warehouse.

The place smelled of must and mildew. She didn't
know what it had housed when it had been in use, but
metal racks remained. Row after row of them, reaching to the rafters, square skeletons that were the
framework for rodent high-rises.

"Mr. Denton?" Maddie called, trying to see
through the dust and dimness as her heart beat a fas-

ter and faster pace with every step that drew them deeper inside, with every passing moment that seemed as if it might bring Bent Nose lurching out of the shadows. That was, if Harry Denton was Bent Nose.

"What if he doesn't show up?" she whispered to Logan as they made their way slowly down the center aisle into the middle of the cavelike structure.

But he didn't answer her. She wasn't even sure he'd heard her or was any more than peripherally aware of her there next to him as he scanned through the dusk.

Maddie's mouth was dry. Very dry.

Things really had gone crazy, she thought. First she'd found herself in someone else's body, now in a place she'd never in a million years thought to be, or would ever have ventured—skulking through an abandoned warehouse to meet a man who was willfully doing harm to someone else.

"So much for romping with the rich and famous," she murmured under her breath. Then, louder, she called, "Are you here, Mr. Denton?"

But the only answer was the echo of her own voice and a responding rocket of birds through the holes in the roof.

Then into the opening at the loading dock stepped a man.

Maddie jumped slightly at the sudden appearance, and Logan shot a hand to steady her.

"Mr. Denton? Is that you?" she asked, hating the shaky sound of her voice. "It's me, Madeline Van Waltonscot."

Silhouetted by the light from outside, it was impossible to see anything but his bulk. He was probably six feet tall and weighed nearly three hundred pounds.

His size alone unnerved her even more until she realized Logan was taller than that, and that while he didn't match the other man's girth, he also didn't have the fleshy, flabby softness that she remembered Bent Nose having, if this was Bent Nose, which she was reasonably sure of by then.

"Who's he?" the man demanded, his voice gruff both in tone and timbre, a suspicious giant who'd smoked too many cigarettes.

"A friend," she answered.

He made an unpleasant sound that was probably supposed to be a laugh. "A friend," he repeated sarcastically. "Lady, who do you think you're kidding? I can smell a cop a mile away."

"He's not a cop. Not anymore. He's—"

"I'm her bodyguard," Logan interjected in a warning tone.

"And he's also helping me piece things together since the accident. I lost a lot of my memory and..." She sighed. She and Logan were still standing in the middle of the warehouse and Harry Denton was some distance away, more on the dock than inside. "Could you come all the way in so we can talk?"

"I don't think so."

Maddie took a few steps in his direction, but both Logan's hand at her arm and Harry Denton's command to stay put stopped her.

From his position of advantage with the light behind him, the hulk glanced from one side to the other of the loading dock as if to see if someone might be coming from either direction, and Maddie glimpsed the long, bulbous bent nose she was familiar with from his brief visit to her in the hospital.

"All right," she said agreeably. "I won't move and you don't have to, either. But could you answer a few questions for me?" She didn't wait for him to respond, going on as if her time were limited. "I know I hired you to discourage someone from bothering me," she repeated what Logan had told her about Madeline Van Waltonscot's request of Quinn. "What I can't remember is who was doing the bothering and why."

"I don't know what you're talking about," Harry Denton said facetiously.

"You must. I know from what you said on the phone that you're the person who's been sending those notes about getting people fired and having their license revoked. I just need my memory refreshed a little."

"Yeah, right."

"Can you at least tell me if it's my brother Steven who I hired you to discourage? And where he is?"

"I told you, I don't know what you're talking about," he repeated even more snidely than before.

"Please, Mr. Denton, this is silly. We can all go to a coffee shop, sit down like civilized people and sort through everything. I promise I'm telling you the truth, and you're not in trouble or going to get in trouble. I just need to know some things."

"Think I was born yesterday, don't you? I'm guessing you got your neck in a noose somehow and you're looking to cut a deal by dragging me in. Well, it isn't going to work. I don't know anything and I'm not saying anything."

Logan's hand at her arm again relayed the message that this wasn't working and not to bother going on with it. Then he spoke. "If you won't tell us anything, at least listen. You need to stop whatever it is you were hired to do."

"Yes!" Maddie added zealously, having momentarily forgotten about that part of needing to meet with this man. "Please, don't do anything else. I'll pay you whatever I agreed to, but just stop. And if you could only send me one more anonymous note with an address or a phone number for whoever it is you've done things to already—"

"Oh, sure, like I'm going to fall for that."

"There's nothing to fall for," Logan said with authority. "Miss Van Waltonscot has had a change of heart and that's all there is to it."

"She hire you, is that it?"

"Not to do whatever it is I hired you to do," Maddie said in a hurry, her voice high and loud with frustration. "I don't want anyone to do the things you've been doing. And I want to make up for what's already been done, if you'd just—"

"I don't know what your game is, lady, but I don't like it."

"No game," Logan said. "Just stop what you're doing."

"Can't stop what I never started," he retorted like a cocky schoolyard bully.

He suddenly raised his arm, and from right above them one of the racks let out a metallic screech.

Maddie barely glanced up to see it teetering back and forth. Then it seemed to hover, as if it might not fall after all. Or maybe it was only a trick of the shadows because suddenly there it was, bearing down on them.

She felt Logan's hand grab her arm in a hard, urgent grip as he yanked her forward, half pulling, half dragging her the rest of the way down the aisle and out the loading-dock door where Harry Denton no longer stood.

A split second after they'd reached it, the rack crashed to the floor, sending clouds of dust billowing into the air, and even the loading dock quivered with the force of it.

"Are you all right?" Logan asked her.

She was but it took her a moment to find her voice to answer him. "I will be as soon as my heart stops doing triple time. You?"

"Fine." Somewhere along the way his hands had taken both of her arms in a firm grasp, but her reassurance that she was unhurt caused him to let her go. "Stay here."

Taking out his gun, he searched the dock from one end to the other and looked up both alleys. But there wasn't a single sign of the other detective or which direction he might have gone.

"He was lying, you know," Maddie said when Logan seemed satisfied that Harry Denton was nowhere around and came back, the gun once more out of sight. "He knows what's going on and he's the one doing those things in the notes. He said as much on the phone."

"I know he is. But he isn't going to admit it, he thinks he's being set up to take a fall."

"Will he at least stop, do you think?"

"Probably."

Then something else occurred to her. "What if he does, but then comes after me because he thinks I tried to double-cross him or something?"

"I don't think that will happen. My bet is he'll give you a wide berth. But if he comes back, I'll deal with him."

She knew he would, too. But still it felt good to have him take her arm again and squeeze it for emphasis.

"Let's get out of here," he suggested, slipping his grip down to hold her hand and heading for the alley on the east side.

But once they rounded the corner of the warehouse onto Wasser Street, Logan stopped cold.

"What?" Maddie said in instant alarm before she caught sight of the same thing he had.

There, parked at the curb where they'd left it, was his Jeep. Only now the hood was up and the engine was spurting loose wires.

Like the falling rack, this, too, was no doubt compliments of Harry Denton and whoever he'd had in the warehouse rafters to help him, stranding Maddie and Logan with a second taste of the havoc he'd been wreaking on someone else on Madeline Van Waltonscot's behalf.

IT TOOK LOGAN an hour to reconnect the wires. He didn't talk as he worked, except to direct Maddie as she held the flashlight.

She wondered if he was angry with her, even though he'd assured her he wasn't each time she'd asked.

When Logan finally managed to get the engine started and they were on their way, he didn't head southeast toward the Van Waltonscot estate. Instead, without saying a word to her about it, he took the Spear Boulevard Viaduct north out of downtown Denver.

"Where are we going?" she ventured.

He looked at her out of the corner of his eye and smiled just a little—the first one she'd seen since their escape from the warehouse.

"I don't know how cozy it is, but I thought I'd take you to a place where you can sit on the floor, eat pizza and watch TV. Unless you have other plans."

His tone was amiable, as if he'd put the past few hours behind him, and it finally allowed her to do the same, chasing away her guilt in the process.

The Strummel property was only ten minutes out of the city. When they got there the main house that Maddie had been to twice before was all dark. Logan pulled into the drive that ran alongside and went all the way back to the carriage house, passing the backyard along the way.

It was lit by ground lights that surrounded a brick-paved patio beneath a canopy of oak and elm trees. The leaves were awash with the brilliant gold and warm red splendor of a rich autumn, and at the moment there were wooden folding chairs forming two sections on either side of a white runner that led from the house to a trellis arch at the farthest end of the patio.

"My brother Quinn is getting married tomorrow evening," Logan offered as he pushed a button that opened the garage door and drove into the empty space. "I was going to talk to you about it tonight."

He turned off the engine and got out. Maddie didn't wait for him to open her door and instead met him halfway.

He went on as if there hadn't been a break in what he'd been saying. "We'll have to put your case on hold for a day. I'm going to need tomorrow to help with wedding things."

Maddie felt her heart sink at the thought of going a full day without seeing him but she put a good face on it. "It's Saturday, anyway. I didn't really expect you to work."

Logan led the way up the stairs at one side of the garage and unlocked a door at the top. He turned a light on inside but held the door for Maddie to go in ahead of him.

"I'd like you to be my date," he said as he followed her. "Unless, of course, you're opposed to getting out of your jeans for that, too," he teased.

She could think of a lot of reasons she'd get out of her jeans for him but she didn't say that. "I think I could be persuaded," she said as if the fact that he was inviting her for something that was purely social didn't please her no end.

He leaned very near to her ear. "I'll work on it then."

Maddie gave him her best smile and pivoted on her heels so she could take a real look at his apartment.

From behind her Logan said, "I'm starved. While I order the pizza why don't you make yourself at home?"

She didn't need any more encouragement than that. She discarded the wool blazer she wore and kicked off her new loafers so that she was down to her stocking feet, her jeans and a V-neck T-shirt.

"Nice place," she called to Logan as she took a quick tour of the large living room with its overstuffed green-plaid couch and chair, big television set and elaborate stereo system.

Then she peeked down a hall to what looked to be two bedrooms and the bathroom before going in the opposite direction to peer over a bar counter into a fair-size kitchen with a claw-footed table just beyond oak cupboards and white appliances.

All in all, the place had the appearance of being well lived in, comfortable and cozier than he'd given it credit for. And as Maddie turned back to the living room, she decided that even with almost no knick-knacks, lots of remote controls and sports magazines and just enough clutter to tell that Logan wasn't meticulous, the apartment was far more homey than the Van Waltonscot mansion.

It also didn't hurt anything that the clean, crisp, citrus scent of his after-shave lingered in the air, claiming the place distinctly as his.

From out of sight in the kitchen Maddie heard a cork pop, and then Logan joined her, carrying two goblets by their stems and a bottle of burgundy.

He handed her the first glass he filled, and while he poured the second for himself she wandered to a table in the corner of the room where a chess board shared space with several framed photographs.

Having no interest in chess, she studied the pictures.

There was Logan looking proud in his police uniform in one photo. He and Quinn together, both in dress blues, their hats under their arms in another. There was a posed portrait of an older couple—his parents, no doubt—and others of people even older, grandparents. There was one of a bunch of men in football uniforms about to tackle another player just out ahead of them with the ball, and when Maddie looked closer she could tell the player with the ball was a much younger Logan, wearing the uniform of the University of Colorado. And there was also a picture of Logan and a very attractive woman against the backdrop of a snowy mountain, both of them in ski clothes, each with an arm around the other's waist.

It was that photograph Maddie picked up to stare more closely at, reminding herself she didn't have any right to feel jealous, but feeling it all the same.

"I didn't know you liked to ski," she said, as if that was what was of interest to her.

"Love it," he confessed.

"I've never been." She held up the snapshot. "Is this your ski partner?"

He grinned at her as if he knew exactly what she was fishing for. "Yes, as a matter of fact she is."

"She's pretty," Maddie granted, setting it back with the others and wishing the compliment hadn't come out so tightly.

"She's also my sister Lindsey."

He'd taken his sweet time getting that out and enjoyed keeping her guessing. Maddie's rejoinder was quick to retrieve some lost ground. "I thought she might be. There's a resemblance." Which was true, now that she took a second glance. She'd just been too lost in jealous assumptions to realize it before.

But now that the subject had been broached...

"Did you have to take your sister to the prom, too?" she teased him as she joined him on the sofa—not too close, though.

"No, I actually got a date on my own, but it took half a dozen turndowns to do it," he played along.

"But now it's skiing with your sister or nobody. Or is there one special woman I've been keeping you from this week?"

"Just one?"

"More than one?"

"Hundreds," he joked with a wry laugh.

But as she sat there looking at him, his incredible handsomeness struck her all over again and she didn't doubt that it was possible.

He'd taken off his jacket, and the holster and gun had disappeared somewhere, too. His collar button was open, his sleeves were rolled to just below his elbows, leaving thick forearms and wrists bare; and his thighs stretched the denim of his jeans so magnificently she yearned to see them unleashed.

But more attractive than the perfection of his face and body was the fact that he didn't seem aware of any of it or of the effect it had on mere mortal women. Which only made him all the more appealing.

A doorbell rang just then and Logan set his wine on the table to answer it somewhere in the kitchen. Maddie assumed there must be an outside entrance there.

When he came back he was carrying a pizza box balanced with plates, napkins and silverware.

Together they set everything out on the low coffee table. Then Logan swept a dramatic hand toward the tan shag carpet and said, "The floor awaits you. Should I turn on the television?"

Maddie sat at one end of the coffee table. "I'd rather talk. Unless there's something you wanted to watch."

"Talking is good. I just didn't want to ruin your idea of a perfect evening," he teased, dropping to a spot around the corner of the table from her.

"I'm betting the story of the women in your life is more interesting," she said, nudging for the information he'd avoided giving before.

"You'd lose that bet," he said as they began to eat.

"What does that mean? You have a boring love life?" she goaded.

"What I have is a busy life that hasn't left a lot of time for romance. And being a cop, well, it's tough on relationships and marriages. I've had to be pretty cautious about who I get involved with because not many women can handle the stress of it."

"Do you speak from experience?"

"Mmm," he said as he finished his first slice of pizza and took another. "I was engaged a few years ago."

One slice of pizza was plenty for Maddie, and since she was through with it, she pushed her plate away. "And something bad happened to blow the relationship to smithereens?" she guessed.

He laughed. "*Smithereens?* Do real people use words like that?"

"What am I? An imitation person?"

He took a moment to study her, looking her up and down and then grinning as if he liked what he'd found. "No, seems like you're a real person who uses words like *smithereens,*" he finally said. "Actually, it was me who was almost blown to smithereens. I took a bullet in the leg when my partner and I broke up a robbery attempt. My fiancée hadn't been comfortable with what my job entailed up to then, and when that happened she just decided she couldn't take it."

"I'm sorry," Maddie said, genuinely meaning it, even though she would hate it if she were sitting across from a married man, enjoying his company as much as she was at that moment.

Logan shrugged. "It was hard at the time. But there's been a lot of water under the bridge since then and I'm okay with it. In fact," he added pointedly, delving into her eyes with those smoldering gray ones of his, "I've come to see it as something that happened for the best."

He only alluded to the fact that he felt that way at that moment because of her, but still it couldn't have delighted her more.

Then he pushed his dish away, too, finished his wine and angled in her direction, raising a knee to brace one of those strong forearms. "What about you? Were you married back in Kansas?"

"No," she said with a laugh. "Not even close. I was lucky to have a date for New Year's Eve. In fact, I rarely did."

"The men of Kansas must be idiots."

"Oh, sure, you say that now, looking at this face and body." And he did, too, this time giving her what seemed to be an involuntary once-over. "But Maggie Morgan did not look like this."

"I know. I saw a picture at Designs Unlimited and my statement stands—if you didn't have dates lined up around the block, the men of Kansas are idiots."

Okay, so maybe she could be more delighted. Especially since he was so sincere she didn't doubt that he meant it.

"Didn't you ever get close to anyone?" he asked then, apparently as curious about her personal history as she'd been about his.

"My limited experience as half of a couple was with one guy in college and another about a year and a half ago, but those relationships both just fizzled. Maybe that was part of the grand design, too. Because if I'd married either one of them I wouldn't be here," she said with a shrug.

Logan was watching her very intently, his expression unreadable. But something had changed along the course of their conversation, or maybe because they were both so relaxed sitting there on the floor, without servants lurking nearby. There seemed to be a new closeness in the air.

"I'm glad you are here," he said, reaching to cup the back of her head, to tease her scalp with a scintillatingly gentle stroke.

"So am I," she admitted simply.

This was all a fantasy come true for Maggie Morgan, she realized as she took in the chiseled planes of Logan's face, the thick shiny hair, the broad shoulders. She'd been so absorbed in this new life and the predicament that had come with it, she hadn't thought about it before, but here she was, alone with a man who was not only gorgeous, he was kind and understanding, genuinely nice, charming, fun to be with and sexier than anyone she'd ever encountered.

And he was as attracted to her as she was to him, but not only because of the way she looked, she knew. He wanted her as much for what she was on the inside as for what was on the outside.

He leaned forward enough to capture her lips with his in a kiss that was tentative at first. But only for a little while before he deepened it, before his lips parted, urging hers open, too.

Maddie closed her eyes and gave herself over to that kiss with a surrender more complete than she'd ever known before.

His tongue came to play and she met it, matched it, played along eagerly. She knew she shouldn't, knew she should pull away. her life was complicated enough and it was just beginning to be sorted through.

But at that moment she only cared about one thing—Logan and what was going on between them.

Somehow he'd moved to take her into his arms, and she let hers wrap around him, filling her hands with the hardness of his back, riding the shifts of hard muscles, clinging to him as he laid her down on the floor and stretched out beside her.

One of his hands cupped the side of her face in a slow, gentle caress that smoothed its way into her hair, learned the curve of her cheekbone and glided down to her jaw.

Still he kissed her, deeper now, with a hunger that Maddie understood because she felt it herself. A hunger tantalized by those all too brief kisses of nights past. A hunger that made her glad when she felt his hand move to the side of her neck, to her collarbone.

She raised her own hands into his hair, holding him to the kiss that was illuminating glittering jewels all along her insides, tiny sparkling gems of pleasure.

She teased his ears with her fingertips, traced his sharp jawbone, all the while accepting every thrust of his tongue, answering each one in kind.

His neck was strong and corded, and she followed the length of it into his collar, trailing around to his nape and wishing she could shuck that shirt and feel the breadth of his bare back against her palms.

She was wishing other things, too. That they could go on kissing like this all night. That there weren't any clothes at all separating them. That that big, powerful hand of his would keep moving lower...

Then it did, slowly, building her anticipation by slow measure in a path that coursed along her side.

But it went all the way to her hip.

She felt a moment's disappointment before he pulled her closer to the length of him, where she could feel just how complete was his desire for her, and disappointment turned instead into a renewed longing for him.

In fact, she wanted him so much she found the courage to slide her own hands down his chest, following the curve of his pectorals, to pull his shirt free of his waistband and indulge in what she'd been longing for—slipping her hands underneath to his back.

Glorious. It really was. Harder, more defined than she'd imagined as she'd studied it through his clothes. His skin was hot, supple, silky. In fact, it felt so wonderful she almost forgot about wanting his hands on her breasts.

Which was just when he followed her lead and pulled the tail of her T-shirt loose to reach beneath it. His hand was slightly callused to a smooth, tough texture, but his touch was light, tender, incredible . . .

He ended their kiss to drop slow, titillating ones to her chin, to the sensitive underside of it, down the column of her neck to the hollow of her throat and then up again.

Maddie's head fell back as he did a delicious torment to her ear, gently biting her lobe, flicking his tongue inside and making her giggle and groan at once.

And then that gifted hand at her naked side began to inch its way up.

Finally! she almost cried out.

The confines of her bra seemed too tight and she longed to be free of it. He made quick work of the front snap and the lacy fabric fell away with the aid of that seeking palm that eased those last few centimeters to cover her yearning, straining nipple at last.

Maddie's breath caught as the exquisite sensation turned those jewels of delight into sparkling diamond pinpoints.

It felt so good. So great.

She couldn't help arching her back, moaning softly as he kneaded, circled, teased, learned every contour.

And yet, as wondrous as it felt, she wanted so much more.

She wanted to be rid of all the clothes that separated them. She wanted to learn each inch of his body. She wanted him to learn each inch of this one that was hers now. And she wanted to know what it felt like when he did.

She wanted him to make love to her.

And she wanted it all so much nothing else mattered.

But that kind of passion, that kind of need, was something she'd never known before. And suddenly it frightened her more than anything that had happened to her since she'd awakened from the coma, leaving her too unnerved to go through with it.

"Logan..." she whispered, her tone somehow echoing the turmoil going on inside of her.

He stopped instantly, lowering his hand to her stomach, halting midway through nibbling her ear.

"Maddie?"

"I want to do this, but I'm not sure...I'm afraid I want it too much."

"Too much?" he repeated as if she'd confused him.

"Maybe too much to think straight."

He chuckled slightly and drew his hand out from under her shirt to press her head to his chest and just hold her instead.

She didn't try to explain because she couldn't, she wasn't sure she understood it herself.

But as she lay there in his arms appreciating that he hadn't gotten angry with her earlier over the warehouse incident or now for ending prematurely what she'd been encouraging, she began to realize that she just might be falling in love with this man who weathered it all with her so patiently.

But lying together couldn't go on long without rekindling what they'd been doing, so after a few minutes Logan let go of her and sat up, taking her with him.

"I think I'd better get you home," he said as if they'd just shared nothing more than pizza and wine.

"Guess this sitting on the floor thing is more dangerous than I thought," she joked. As he got up, she used that moment to refasten her bra and then accepted his hand to help her to her feet, too.

"Everything seems to be dangerous when the two of us get together," he said. "Why do you suppose that is?"

She shrugged. "Maybe because there are feelings involved?"

He smiled down at her, a smile that was so warm, so sweet, so penetrating, it filled her with warm honey. "There are definitely feelings involved. And growing by the minute. Much as I keep trying to control them."

But the feelings wouldn't be controlled, and somehow Maddie knew it. Hers wouldn't. His wouldn't.

Oh, maybe she'd managed to stop what had come out of those feelings again tonight. But standing there, looking up into Logan's face, aware of the swell of her heart, she knew the feelings couldn't be denied for much longer. That they would have their day. In spite of everything else that was going on. Because he was right, they were growing by the minute. All on their own.

Logan took a deep breath and jammed his shirt-tails into his jeans with quick, harsh jabs. "Come on. Let's get you home," he repeated, and then they both went through the steps needed to wrap up the evening.

But leaving that apartment a few moments later was by far the hardest thing Maddie had had to do since coming to grips with the fact that she wasn't herself anymore.

Because now that the pure power of the passion they shared wasn't scaring her so much, she knew that what she really wanted was to stay the night with Logan.

And that until she did, she wouldn't feel complete.

Chapter Seven

"Is your bag packed?" Logan asked in greeting as Maddie opened the front door late the following afternoon.

He came into the house like a maelstrom. She didn't know if his agitation and the sense of urgency about him was because he was now rushed for time, or if it was due to the message she'd found on her answering machine when she'd returned from buying a gift.

"Yes, I packed a bag," she answered, pointing to the spot near the staircase where it waited. "But are you sure I really need to hide out? I mean, this house is full of people day and night. It isn't as if I'd be on my own should—"

"This house is full of people who cook and clean and do laundry, not people who are here to protect you. It's safer for them, too, to close up the house until this thing is over."

"But there wasn't an overt threat—"

"It wasn't only what he said. I didn't like his tone. Whoever it is sounds desperate. And desperation breeds some pretty ugly things."

The unidentified message from the same man who'd called before had sent chills up Maddie's spine when she'd first heard it. But since calling Logan and having him insist that she stay at his place, where he could keep a constant watch over her, she'd had chills of an entirely different sort and she wasn't sure what was the most dangerous—ambiguous threats from a mystery man or having once again to resist her attraction to Logan.

"Do you have the tape with you?" he asked as he picked up the suitcase near the steps. "I want to listen to it again on the way home to make sure I didn't miss anything hearing it over the phone."

"It's in my purse," she said, retrieving the tape along with the hanger that held the simple teal green dress she'd chosen to wear to the wedding. "Bernice is waiting for everyone to leave and then she'll lock up, so we can go if you need to get right back. I'm sorry this happened today, when you had so many other things to do."

"I just want you out of here."

He was definitely in a protective mode because he went out ahead of her, blocking her path while he looked around and only letting her across the threshold when he was convinced no one was lurking outside. Then he stayed right beside her, his hand at the ready at her arm, as they went to a vehicle Maddie hadn't seen before—a station wagon with tinted windows and two child carriers in the back seat.

"*This* is the getaway car?" she joked to ease the tension.

He smiled as he ushered her into the passenger side. "It's my sister's. She and her family are already at the house, and one of the twins she and her new husband are in the process of adopting threw my keys in the bushes. So I took the diapermobile while she searched for them."

He shut and locked the door and then went around to the driver's side.

Maddie had the tape ready for him when he got in. He listened to it three times in succession as he drove, all the while keeping a wary eye on his rearview mirror and the cars around them.

"How could you do this?" the distraught voice said from the tape player in the dashboard. "I ask for your help and you destroy us. You take the hell our life is in right now and make it worse. That's evil. You're evil. No soul. No conscience. And I just have one thing to say to you. Somehow, someway, I'm going to hurt you back, Madeline. I swear to God, I'm going to hurt you back. You'd better be looking over your shoulder and sleeping with the lights on."

Okay, so maybe it wasn't ambiguous, after all.

When Logan clicked off the tape deck, Maddie said, "Do you think Harry Denton did something after we saw him yesterday—even though we told him not to— and that's what inspired this call?"

"No, I don't. But that doesn't mean he hadn't done something between the time he wrote the last note and when we saw him in the warehouse. It also doesn't mean there haven't been other repercussions from what he did before."

"Evil," Maddie repeated more to herself than to Logan. "I don't think I like getting a second chance at life as someone who's evil.

"I can't believe the timing of these calls," she went on. "If only I'd been there to pick up even one of them. Or to have the phone company trace them, we'd know who we're looking for."

Logan must have heard the depth to which this incident had shaken her. He reached over and squeezed her nape reassuringly, and his own agitation seemed to give way to concern for her. "We'll find this guy."

"Or he'll find us."

"Not today he won't. We'll be safely in the bosom of family and friends, and I'll be watching you like a hawk," he told her with a devilish grin that said his surveillance wouldn't be completely professional. "Let's just try to relax and enjoy ourselves as much as we can, huh? We've both earned it."

He pulled off the highway just then, and since theirs was the only car to take the exit and the only one anywhere around all the way to the Strummel home, Maddie found it easier to put at least any imminent threat of danger out of her mind.

Besides, being with Logan made her feel safe, and as they drove into the driveway she decided to give in to that and to try pushing back on the increasingly disturbing thoughts of being Madeline Van Waltonscot.

"Quinn will be upstairs getting dressed," Logan explained as they gathered her things to take to his apartment. "His bride-to-be is using the main house. I'll change, and then he and I need to have pictures taken so we'll leave the place to you. Will that work out?"

"Sure."

At the top of the stairway he opened the door and called inside, "Quinn? Are you decent?"

"Yeah."

Logan's manners took the forefront again and he waited for Maddie to go in first. His brother was standing at a mirror on the hall wall directly across from the door, dressed in a tuxedo. He didn't turn to greet them; instead he went on cussing as he tried and failed to tie his tie.

"I'll put your things in the guest room and be out shortly," Logan said to Maddie as the rush seemed to be on again.

Since she'd had the distinct impression on their one previous meeting that his brother didn't like her, she wasn't thrilled about being left alone with him now. But there she was.

"Nervous?" she asked amiably to break the ice.

"I didn't think so. But I can't get this damn thing tied so I must be."

Maddie set down her purse and draped her dress over the back of the sofa. "I'm an expert bow-tie tier. Want some help?"

He glanced at her in the mirror, his expression skeptical. But he seemed at wit's end so he said, "Okay. Why not?"

He came into the living room and stood in front of her as if he were facing a firing squad. "How did you get to be an expert bow-tie tier?" he asked.

"My dad wore nothing but. In our town back in Kansas he was famous for wearing them. Polka dots, stars, trout, stripes—he loved being known as the minister who wore wild bow ties. Of course it embarrassed me to death as a kid, but he'd tease me and cajole me into tying the dumb things for him." The memory clutched at her heart. "I'd give anything to have him back now, outrageous bow ties and all."

Quinn didn't say anything. Not that she'd expected him to. But when she finished with the tie and looked up at his face she found more of that skepticism.

"Ah, I forgot. You don't believe I'm not really Madeline Van Waltonscot, do you?" she said, knowing Logan had told her story to his brother.

Quinn didn't respond again, instead moving back to the mirror to assess the job she'd done. But the arch of his eyebrows told her she'd surprised him with the skill of her work. "Thanks," he said, pressing the tie against his throat and cocking his head this way and that to look at it, as if he expected to find flaws.

When he didn't, he looked down the hall and called, "Get a move on, Logan. We're running late." Then he had no choice but to come back into the living room to wait with Maddie.

He didn't seem inclined to make conversation, and she hated sitting there in silence with him. So she went on talking about her family, who were very much on her mind suddenly.

"My mother, on the other hand, made brownies like no one else in the world. The problem was, while she did it she sang. Loud and really, really bad. A couple of times she didn't realize I'd brought a friend in, and there she'd be, belting out 'Amazing Grace,' off-key and screeching, and I'd be mortified."

Quinn was staring at her, studying her like a virus in a petri dish, but still he didn't make any comment.

"Not that any of this matters to you," she went on, anyway. "I know I'm just rambling. But I've been thinking this afternoon that I didn't come from people who willfully did harm to anyone else, and I guess I'm having some trouble coming to grips with how anyone could. With my family, that's as bad as it got—tacky neck wear and lousy singing. Pretty mild stuff compared to what I've found myself in recently." She shrugged. "I guess maybe that's what's making me miss them both today. And my own life, too, for that matter. There might not have been money and social position, but there wasn't any cruelty, either."

"Your own life," Quinn repeated, perching on the arm of the overstuffed chair.

"Doubting Thomas," she accused with a laugh. "I know. You're thinking that if the body switch is true, why wouldn't I be happy as a lark about getting what most people—myself included—wished for. More money than I'll ever be able to spend. A mansion. A staff that waits on me hand and foot. A life straight out of a nighttime soap opera. But it isn't all it's cracked up to be. And I'm a fish out of water in it."

"You'll get used to it," he murmured wryly.

"Will I? I wonder. And even if I do or if I ever manage to change it to a more normal way of living, I'm still stuck being that person, that woman who would hire someone to do awful things to other people. Will I be able to get used to that?"

Once more he didn't answer her. He only went on watching her just the way Logan was wont to do.

Maddie took a deep breath and sighed, hating the melancholy feelings this newest message had left her with today. Feelings that had somehow driven her to confide in a person who refused to believe her.

Oh, well. One more oddity to add to the list.

She suddenly wanted to escape this Strummel's scrutiny and began to gather what must have been the clothes Quinn had worn over to the apartment—a sweat suit, tennis shoes, white athletic socks.

"So, enough about my identity crisis," she said with renewed vigor. "Where are you going for your honeymoon?"

"A cabin we own in the mountains."

"Oh, I'd love that! Fresh air and the aspens all turning color. Maybe you'll get lucky and it'll snow."

"I don't suppose it compares to the French Riviera or Acapulco or a cruise on a private yacht," he said pointedly.

"Sure, those trips would be nice, too, but I'd be just as happy in the mountains."

She'd folded the clothes and set them on the seat cushion of the chair he was on. As she did she noticed a smudge on one of his brightly polished shoes. "Let me get that," she said, using one of the socks to rub at it until it was gone. "There. That's better. A groom has to have a well-tied tie and flawlessly shiny shoes—it's a law."

When she straightened up again she found a new expression on Quinn Strummel's face, one that seemed perplexed and amazed at once.

"What?" Maddie asked.

He laughed slightly. "Maybe you *aren't* Madeline Van Waltonscot."

A small wave of that melancholia washed over her again at that. "The trouble is, I don't have a choice. I have to be."

THE YARD between the carriage house and Quinn's place was brightly lit by candles and full of bouquets of white roses sprigged with baby's breath. By six o'clock all the guests were seated and the service began, uniting Quinn Strummel with Cara Walsh, who made a lovely bride in antique satin and lace. Lindsey was the matron of honor, and Logan the best man.

But as he stood just outside the trellis arch he couldn't help keeping one eye on the ceremony and the other on Maddie where she sat with the rest of the family—Cara's wheelchair-bound grandmother, Lindsey's new husband Graham and their twins, and Graham's mother.

Not that Logan was worried something was going to happen to her here, tonight, in the crispness of the early autumn air. He just couldn't seem to keep from looking at her at every opportunity.

After all, he thought she was the most beautiful woman there, dressed in a short teal green, spaghetti-strapped sheath with a beaded bolero jacket hiding her soft, pale shoulders, and her long, silky ebony hair falling straight down her back.

And she was his.

Well, maybe not technically, but for tonight's festivities, anyway.

And nothing made him happier than that thought as he stood there witnessing his brother's marriage.

The gathering of family, friends and neighbors was small, which made the receiving line a quick proposition when the service was over. Then Logan was free to be with Maddie for the rest of the evening. And if he'd had any lingering doubts that Maddie really was Maddie and not Madeline Van Waltonscot, that evening would have dispelled them.

From helping to move chairs so there could be dancing on the patio, to bringing Cara's grandmother up-to-date on the latest home adaptations available to help the handicapped, to giving the twins horsey rides on her ankles, to telling Graham which of the types of tennis shoes he manufactured were her favorites, she was down-to-earth, personable and not for a single second the heiress mingling with the masses. Instead she was every inch the Kansas-bred minister's daughter kicking off her satin pumps to dance in her stocking feet and delight in the party and everyone there.

"She polished my shoe."

Logan was sitting at one of the tables watching Maddie dance with the teenage boy who lived next door when Quinn's voice came from behind him. He jerked as if he'd been pulled from a trance and switched his attention to his brother as Quinn sat down.

"Who polished your shoe?"

Quinn poked his chin in Maddie's direction. "Your client. The woman you're sitting here devouring with your eyes."

"When did she do that?"

"While you were putting on your tux."

"Bet it surprised you."

"Shocked the hell out of me. And I'd been giving her a hard time up until then, too. Not being very sympathetic to her even though she seemed sort of upset. She was talking about her father the minister and her mother and something about cruelty that I didn't quite understand."

Logan filled him in on the latest message.

"It seems to have disturbed her. She said she was having an identity crisis. I thought it was a little late for that. Wouldn't it have set in immediately if she really did wake up and find herself inhabiting someone else's body?"

"She's had a lot to deal with—external things. Could be that addressing the internal issues is just starting. I expect that when everything is over and she has to accept actually living life as Madeline Van Waltonscot, she'll have a whole lot more to contend with in the way of adjusting to it. At least that's my armchair analysis, for what's it worth."

Logan looked back toward the patio dance floor at Maddie, and Quinn's gaze seemed to follow.

"I wanted you to know that as crazy as it sounds, I'm beginning to change my mind about her," Quinn admitted.

Logan laughed. "There's none of the heiress in her, is there?"

"No, there doesn't seem to be. As hard as that is for me to believe. But you'd still better be careful. Actually, I think you'd better be *more* careful. You're right that when the case is solved and she has to get down to everyday living she's going to have a lot to hash through emotionally—I saw some of it earlier."

Quinn stood and slapped Logan on the back, but Logan didn't respond to his brother's warning or even take his eyes off Maddie.

Instead he was lost in wonder at how genuinely beautiful she was. More beautiful with every day that passed, he thought. The Madeline Van Waltonscot of before the accident had been physically beautiful, but it had been only skin deep. Now beauty seemed to radiate from the core of her, the kind of beauty that would have transformed even the less attractive Maggie Morgan.

And as he sat there watching her charm the shy teenager who was clearly infatuated, Logan started to think about his own feelings for her.

It was time he stopped fooling himself and admitted that he'd never be successful in resisting his attraction to her or his desires for her.

Because at that moment he realized the indisputable truth that regardless of how much he fought it, regardless of how unwise it might be, he was falling in love with her.

IT WAS MIDNIGHT by the time the last guest, the last caterer, the last musician, was gone. While Logan went to lock the doors on the main house, Maddie padded upstairs to his apartment and peeled off her snagged panty hose to toss into the trash.

It was very cool by then, but she was loath to wear the bolero jacket that completed her ensemble, and even more loath to get into her bathrobe and admit the evening was over. So instead she borrowed a white shirt from the top of a stack of four that appeared to have come from the cleaners and was waiting on Logan's kitchen table to be put away.

She was in the middle of rolling up the long sleeves when he came in. She stood with one bare foot over the other to keep them warm.

"Nice wedding," she told him. "I had a really good time."

"So did I."

He'd shrugged out of his jacket, tie and cummerbund some time ago, his collar was open, his cuffs were turned up twice and his hair was less perfect than it had been at the start of the evening, but he looked terrific just the same.

Maddie feasted on the sight, feeling as if she hadn't had enough of his company yet tonight, what with all the other people around and both of them distracted by the celebration.

"I hope you don't mind that I swiped one of your clean shirts, but it's chilly," she said then, switching feet so that the right now tried warming the left.

Logan noticed, then his gaze did a slow rise up her legs before coming back to her face. "You really are cold," he said, kicking off his shoes, too, and reaching both hands to finger-comb his hair and stretch at the same time. "Want a little brandy to warm your bones? Or would you rather just call it a night?"

"Brandy sounds good," she said because the craving for a few more minutes with him was greater than anything else.

While he was in the kitchen getting the drinks she sat crossways on the couch with her back against the arm, her knees up, the long shirttails wrapped around her legs to maintain her modesty in the short dress and her toes buried between two seat cushions.

"Quinn told me you were down in the dumps earlier," Logan said as he returned with juice glasses half full of the amber liqueur.

"I'm okay," Maddie answered, accepting one of them. "That answering machine message just kind of got to me."

He sat down so near to her that his left leg covered her insteps, propped his feet on the coffee table and angled one arm along the back of the sofa so that his brandy was braced just a few inches from her shoulder. "Even my brother is coming around to believing that you really aren't Madeline Van Waltonscot."

She merely nodded, not wanting to talk about that. Quinn was only one example of what she'd faced since coming out of the coma, what she still had to face—people who disliked her for what the heiress had been and found it impossible to believe that she was any different now.

But tonight the garden wedding, the modest surroundings, the ordinary people had all felt like her old life, and the last thing she wanted was for any of the new one to ruin it. For just a little while longer she wanted to be free of it. Free of all the confusion and tension and trappings.

"I liked your friends and family," she said to change the subject.

"They seemed to like you, too. When my next-door neighbor Paul wasn't getting you to dance with him, he was worshiping you from afar, and I think Lindsey's twins would have rather stayed with you than gone home."

"What can I say? I have a knack with teenage boys and toddlers."

As if he weren't thinking about what he was doing and only answered an urge, Logan clasped one of her ankles and did an unconsciously sensual massage. "Seemed to me it was the man in Paul and not the boy in him that was responding to you tonight."

Maddie laughed. "He was sort of ogling me."

"He has a major crush on you."

"That's a first."

"Actually it's a second. So do I and I beat him to it."

She'd just taken a sip of her brandy, which made it difficult to tell if it was that or Logan's words that sent a wave of warmth all through her. And somewhere along the way her toes had emerged from the seat cushions to snuggle under his thigh.

"It's okay if you have a crush on me," she heard herself say before she'd even thought about it. "Because I have one on you, too."

"Poor Paul will be devastated," Logan said with a grin.

"I'm too old to go to the homecoming dance, anyway," she joked.

"Oh, I don't know—" his hand rose a few inches up her shin "—I've never met a teenage girl who could compare to you. The kid has taste."

Logan's hand left her ankle and came to rest with his palm against her cheek, his fingers curved around the back of her head to pull her toward him. He met her midway in a brandied kiss that was light and playful, but heady just the same, causing her toes to curl up into the solid expanse of his thigh.

The same sensation she'd had the night before of glittering jewels just below the surface of her skin began again, too, warming her more than his shirt or the liquor.

Then he stopped kissing her and drew away only enough to press his chin to her forehead while his thumb did a slow caress of the sensitive spot just behind her ear. "I really did bring you to stay here to keep you safe, not to seduce you," he said in a voice that was low and husky with desire already.

"I never doubted it," she assured him because it was the truth, though she'd known that spending the night in his apartment—or anywhere near him—was tempting fate and their willpower.

"There's a lock on the guest-room door. Maybe you should go there now and use it, because if things get started tonight the way they have before, I don't think I'll be able to stop it."

She thought about that, and about how unnerved she'd been when passion had ignited the past evening, about how worried she'd been that that passion had left her not thinking straight enough to make a decision as important as this one.

But she was very sure she was thinking straight now, when passion was only a tiny ember that could still be controlled. And what she knew was that she wanted to follow her feelings, her instincts, tonight. Feelings that were for Logan. And instincts that told her that being with him, giving in to wanting him so much it hurt, keeping everything else out of her mind the way she'd been doing throughout the wedding celebration, couldn't be wrong.

"Would you *want* to stop?" she asked quietly.

"No. I want to make love to you."

"It's what I want, too," she said even more quietly.

"Be sure, Maddie."

"I am."

He kissed her again, a kiss that would have knocked her socks off if she'd still had them on. A deep kiss that branded her, claimed her as his, and set alight those gems beneath the surface of her skin once more as pinpricks of pleasure.

He went on kissing her. Exploring, teasing with his tongue in slow, lingering kisses. Short pulls of each of her lips between his. Kisses that trailed to her cheekbones, to her chin and down her neck, to her ears where he nibbled and sent chills along her spine.

Maddie reveled in it all, giving herself over to the wonders the man could rouse with his mouth until her whole body was weighted with relaxation, until every sense, every nerve was tuned in to him alone and the leisurely, steady rise of desire he was orchestrating within her.

Somewhere along the way they'd set their brandy glasses down so there was nothing hindering him when he rose from the couch to scoop her up into his arms and carry her to his bedroom.

It seemed clear that he hadn't been expecting tonight to end this way, because although his big king-size bed was made, the clothes he'd worn earlier were scattered haphazardly around.

But Maddie was less aware of that, or even of the antique bureau and general color scheme of brown and bronze dusted by moonglow from the two large windows along one wall, than she was of the stronger scent of his after-shave lingering in the air.

He set her on her feet at the bedside and began kissing her again as his hands slipped under the shirt she'd borrowed and eased it from her shoulders to fall around her bare feet.

Then went the spaghetti straps of her dress, but only to the middle of her arms before he abandoned them and went to work on the buttons of his own shirt.

Maddie helped in that quest because she longed for that big, broad chest to be bare the way she'd been imagining it since meeting the man. When the buttons were all unfastened and he'd pulled the shirttails free, she mimicked his actions, running her palms along his shoulders underneath to finesse it off him.

And once she had, she was driven by the need to see him.

This time she ended their kiss with a few teasers of her own and then feasted her eyes on the glory that was Logan Strummel's bare chest.

And it was glorious.

Hard, honed pectorals gave way to a narrow waist and a tight, flat stomach where a hint of dark hair ran in a straight line from his perfect navel to disappear into his tuxedo pants.

Maddie let her palms ride from the expanse of hugely muscled shoulders to his chest, following the path with small kisses as she felt him lower the zipper of her dress down her back.

She didn't have anything but lace panties on underneath—not because she'd anticipated this, either, but because the dress had a bra built into the front of it. Now her breasts felt ready to burst from inside of it, and the lower that zipper went, the lower her neckline got, too, as the upper swells seemed to burgeon eagerly nearer the top of it.

But not for long before he sent the green sheath to join the shirts on the floor. Then those big, powerful hands of his followed the same path her hands on him had—from cupping her shoulders to slide across her collarbone and down to her straining, erect nipples.

That first touch took her breath away in a gasp of pleasure, quieted by his mouth over hers once more.

But it was only a preview of things to come.

He reached around her to fling back the quilt that covered his bed and eased her onto the mattress, where she lay watching him shed the rest of his clothes.

Lord, but the man was magnificent! Roman statues could have been carved in his likeness. And he wanted her. Oh, did he want her! For there for her to see was the long, hard, thick proof of it.

He joined her on the bed, taking her in his arms in the same movement, capturing her mouth with his as he slipped her panties down and away, too, so their naked bodies could finally meet without a barrier.

It felt so incredible, it gave Maddie goose bumps.

But he had better things in store for her than that.

His talented hands found her breasts again, kneading, teasing, arousing her nipples so exquisitely she would have cried out except that his mouth and tongue were keeping her otherwise occupied. And when he deserted it to kiss his way to her breasts and work the magic of his mouth there, the pleasure was so intense she could hardly breathe, let alone make a sound.

Especially when he reached lower with that free hand and awakened her to her need for him even further.

Time stood still as desire coursed through her, built by his hand, his mouth, the way his taut, warm flesh felt beside her, beneath her seeking fingers and caressing palms.

Just when she thought she might die if she didn't have him finally inside of her, he rose above her, finding his place between her legs and slowly, carefully inching himself into that spot that cried out to be completed by him.

This time Maddie couldn't help but groan at the pure wondrousness of that union. She knew she wanted this moment to go on for an eternity, that no matter how many other things might be wrong, this was elegantly, exquisitely right.

Then he began to move. A rhythmic dance that delved into her and out again, first with torturous care, then slowly gaining speed, faster still until urgency drove them to seek that highest point where white-hot ecstasy exploded simultaneously, melding their bodies together and suspending them for a single brief moment of pure, unadulterated bliss that left Maddie clinging to his powerful back and accepting—welcoming joyously—the full length of him into her so deeply it felt as if he really had reached the core of her.

Then slowly, slowly, in waves that teased with the momentary return of tingling pleasure, their climax receded until Logan carefully lowered his full weight onto her and pressed his lips to her temple in one final, sweet kiss.

"I love you, Maddie," he whispered in a passion-ragged voice.

"I love you, too," she answered so, so softly, without even thinking about it, letting the words come straight from her heart.

And that was all either of them said, maybe because no matter what was to come, at that moment it was all that mattered.

After a while Logan slipped from inside her, rolled to his back and moved her to his side where her head rested in the hollow of his shoulder as if it were a pillow specially carved for her. Then he pulled the sheet and blanket over them and settled in to sleep.

As she drifted off herself there in his arms, Maddie had a greater sense of peace and contentment than she'd ever known. And she couldn't help wishing that the new life she'd found herself in never had to intrude on that.

But even in the afterglow of such divine lovemaking, when she'd given her heart to Logan, she had the sinking feeling that it would.

Chapter Eight

The sounds of the cleanup crew on the patio below Logan's apartment woke Maddie early the next morning. She didn't mind. Any more than she'd minded when Logan himself had awakened her to make love to her during the night. She was so glad to be there with him that sleeping through it seemed like a waste of precious time.

He was lying on his back, one arm stretched out underneath her neck where it had been wrapped around her when they'd fallen asleep after the last round of passion, and Maddie was on her side facing his profile. They were bathed in the warm rays of the sun coming in through the curtains they'd forgotten to close, and she lay very still, basking in it and enjoying the sight of Logan as he slept.

His sharp jaw and hollow cheeks were whisker shadowed, his hair was tousled, yet he still looking amazingly, ruggedly handsome. And as she memorized every line, every angle, every skin tone of that face, she realized all over again that she loved him more than seemed possible, especially when she'd been fighting so hard against what was happening between them since they'd met.

Something outside crashed, as if one of the wooden chairs from the wedding had been dropped.

Logan's brows furrowed but his eyes didn't open. "Who the hell called in the cavalry at dawn?" he muttered as he curled his arm around her and pulled her closer.

"Not me," Maddie answered, melding willingly to his side.

He kissed her forehead and murmured like a contented tomcat.

But when he didn't move more than that or make another sound, Maddie thought he'd gone back to sleep.

Then he said, "How about we just stay here in bed forever?"

"That's a good idea. But who's going to make the world go away if we do?"

"Maybe it'll forget about us."

"I'm willing to give it a try," she agreed, snuggling against his hot body. "Until starvation drives me out, anyway."

"You'd throw me over for food?"

"Maybe just one breakfast burrito."

"Heiresses don't eat breakfast burritos."

"You're telling me? I asked for one the other day and the cook nearly had a heart attack. I ended up with a soufflé in a crepe smothered with sherry sauce. It was good but just not the same."

He moaned this time. "Now you're making me hungry."

"Call the cook. I'm sure he'd come over here and fix you one."

He seemed to think about that. "Tough choice," he said after a moment. "A French chef to cook my breakfast or keeping you captive in my bed. Hmm."

She raised her leg over his and slid it up with a slow, lingering caress of her foot along the way.

He looked down at her through hooded eyes. "*You're* the one who started talking about food."

"I think I could probably wait for it, though. A little while longer, anyway."

"I wish you'd make up your mind," he pretended to complain as he slipped his hand under the covers to her naked breast.

"Okay. Food," she teased, trying to roll away from him.

But he didn't let her go. "Later," he whispered in a husky, seductive tone.

Much later as it turned out.

It was nearly noon before they actually got out of bed after making playful, passionate love once more and lingering in each other's arms. But eventually the demands of the day forced them up.

They spent the afternoon at the Van Waltonscot estate deciding on a dress for Maddie to wear to the Unessa Ball that night. With a room-size closet full of gowns fit for a queen, Maddie hadn't seen the purpose of buying something new, so instead she and Logan explored the wealth of options.

In the end she chose a black strapless, sequined floor-length dress that fit like a second skin and was slit up the front of her right leg.

The heiress's jewelry was locked in a safe in the section of the closet that stored the furs. Luckily Maddie had happened upon the combination hidden in the makeup drawer of the dressing table. From the vault she took a six-strand pearl choker and matching bracelet, feeling like a kid playing with her mother's valuables.

There were no new messages on the answering machine or notes from Harry Denton, and so once Maddie had picked a pair of three-inch high heels to go with the gown, she and Logan went back to his place to get ready.

Logan had another black tuxedo to wear, this one more elegant than what he'd worn for the wedding. It lacked the satin stripes down the pant legs, and rather than a peaked lapel, it had a shawl collar.

He looked stunningly handsome when Maddie finished her own dressing and found him waiting for her in his living room.

Apparently she didn't present too shabby a picture herself, for his eyes opened wide at the first glance her way, his brows rose and he got a little slack jawed before he said, "Wow!"

"This dress had a receipt pinned to the inside—as if maybe Madeline Van Waltonscot might not have been sure she was going to keep it. Do you know what it cost? Eight *thousand* dollars," Maddie informed him with a full measure of her own amazement in her voice.

"And worth every penny," he murmured, taking her hand to twirl her slowly around so he could see the full image. "It beats the hell out of blue jeans."

She was about to take issue with that when they heard the sound of a car pulling up the drive.

Logan took a look out the window and confirmed that it was the Van Waltonscot chauffeur-driven limousine—long, white and waxed to such a high sheen moonlight gleamed off it.

Having rejected the assortment of fur pieces she could have chosen from because they were all real and Maddie was opposed to killing animals for their skins, Logan held up the satin stole she'd brought and wrapped it around her bare shoulders. But not before placing a warm kiss to the side of her nape.

"We could stay here," Maddie suggested as if tempting Adam with the apple.

"Not if we ever intend to find out who wants to wring this pretty little neck, we couldn't," he answered in a warm gust of his breath against her skin.

"How about speed interrogating so we can leave early?"

"*Speed interrogating?*"

"We'll ask a lot of questions, really fast so we'll learn what we need to know and can leave."

"Great idea," he deadpanned. "Or we could knock a few heads together and scare people into talking to us." He let go of her shoulders and took her elbow to guide her outside to the landing of the staircase that ran along the side of the carriage house.

"Does knocking heads together and scaring people get fast results?" she asked as if she were considering it, playing along.

"Sure, but do it once and you aren't likely to be invited out again."

"You mean it might actually hurt my social life? Well, we wouldn't want that."

He pulled the door closed as Maddie headed down the steps.

"Still, though," he said when he caught up with her at the bottom, "I think an early departure once we've garnered some information wouldn't be uncalled for so soon after the accident."

Maddie shot him a smile over her shoulder. "A man after my own heart," she muttered.

"Exactly."

They'd reached the car by then, where the chauffeur waited. Maddie asked how he was and about his new baby daughter, and only when she'd insisted he show her a picture of the infant did she and Logan get into the limousine.

"I still think it would have been a hoot to go in the Jeep," she told Logan when the chauffeur had closed them in.

"Maddie," Logan said with a slight roll to his eyes. "Pretend you're Cinderella and just enjoy the splendor of the night."

"That would be a whole lot easier if I was Cinderella, but in this reincarnation I seem to be the horrid stepmother and the evil stepsisters all rolled up into one."

Still, Logan was right about the splendor of the affair, and Maddie couldn't help secretly delighting in it.

When the limousine pulled to a stop in front of the Fairmont Hotel on Seventeenth Street in downtown Denver, there were liveried valets to open the car door, a red carpet from the curb to the hotel entrance and reporters and photographers clustered on either side from every newspaper, magazine, television and radio station she could name.

Inside the hotel's plush red-velvet-arrayed lobby, her outer wrap was whisked away and they were ushered into the ballroom. The table they were taken to seated eight and had a prime location next to the dance floor, but far enough from the musicians to allow undisturbed conversation.

The other three couples already there were Maddie's accountant and his wife, her lawyer and his wife, and the chief executive officer of Scottie's Food Marts—another man well past fifty years old—and his wife.

"Didn't Madeline Van Waltonscot have *any* friends?" Maddie whispered to Logan behind her hand just before they were seated and the amenities began.

They were effectively stuck at the table through the first portion of the evening as a five-course meal was served and no one did any mingling. Trying to get information out of their dinner companions was no more successful in a social setting than it had been in a business one. In fact, it was mainly business that was discussed as all three men did their best to ignore Logan and try to convince Maddie to reconsider her stand against cutbacks on full-time employees.

When the chocolate-torte dessert dishes were finally removed and the music began, Logan asked her to dance and they escaped.

"Ah, sweet rewards," Maddie murmured once she was in Logan's arms.

He smiled down at her and held her close but he was clearly in his work mode because he didn't say anything and spent most of the dance scoping out the other guests.

When the music ended, Maddie became the center of attention as innumerable people began to approach her with well-wishes. But like the cards and notes she'd received when she'd awakened from the coma, the sentiments were perfunctory, formal and brief, robbing her and Logan of the opportunity to ask any questions.

Until a tall, buxom woman with curly white hair and a horsey face approached them.

"I've been waiting for you to come to me, Madeline, but apparently if I want to see you tonight I'd better come to you," she said in an irascible greeting as she looked down a large nose at Maddie.

"I'm sorry," Maddie answered the woman, realizing instantly that this was not only yet another person she should know and didn't, but one who could top the old Madeline Van Waltonscot's imperious attitude.

Logan must have realized it, too, because he took a protective step nearer to her.

She gave the elderly woman a chagrined smile. "I know I know you, but—"

"I'd heard you were having memory problems, but you don't even remember *me?*" the woman asked incredulously.

"I remember your face," Maddie lied.

Logan stepped into the breach, introducing himself, clearly an attempt to inspire the woman to do the same.

It worked, although the only thing he got for his effort was a withering glare before she aimed her response at Maddie. "I'm Miriam Prescott Manderlie, the oldest and closest friend of your family. I was at school with your grandmother and very nearly married your grandfather myself before my head was turned by my dear Malcolm."

"Of course," Maddie said, as if this had sparked her memory.

"How are you feeling," the older woman demanded, "besides being fuzzy-brained?"

"Physically I'm just fine," Maddie assured her.

"I must say I was surprised to return from our summer home in Carmel to hear you can't remember things. I phoned the hospital all the while you were in a coma and consulted with your doctor when you awakened, and there was no mention of this lapse."

"It wasn't evident when I was in the hospital. It was only when I got out that I began to realize there were things—and people—that I couldn't seem to recall."

"Rumor has it that you've been behaving very strangely and don't remember much at all."

This old bear was not going to be so easily fooled.

Again Logan must have recognized it at about the same time Maddie did, and he came to her rescue. "So you've known the Van Waltonscot family for years and years," he mused. "Maybe you could help fill in some of the blanks for Madeline."

Maddie took up where Logan had left off. "I've been particularly bothered by thoughts of Steven. I remember him from when we were children but then I draw a blank."

The older woman was hardly a warm sort, but at the mention of that name she turned into an iceberg and looked at Maddie as if she'd lost not only her memory but her mind. "Steven?" she said as if it left a foul taste in her mouth.

Maddie ignored it and plunged in anyway. "Yes. I'm wondering where he is, why I haven't heard from him."

"Oh, you have knocked something loose," the woman said, so outraged she literally sent her second chin shimmying.

Once more Maddie pretended not to notice. "I'm worried about where he might be. Have you seen him or heard from him?"

"Seen him or heard from him? Absolutely not! That ungrateful, hate-spewing—"

Logan cut her off as if her words shocked him. "Steven hasn't been concerned that his sister was nearly killed?"

"Who knows! No one has had any contact with him in all the years since Madeline's father disinherited him. And rightfully so. Making up those hideous lies. We were all only too glad to have that whole matter ended for good."

"What whole matter?" Maddie asked.

Miriam Prescott Manderlie drew herself up to a height that nearly matched Logan's, aiming another glare his way, as if he had asked that last question instead of Maddie. "This conversation is in poor taste," she announced. Then, to Maddie again, she said, "Come for tea one day soon. I'd be happy to fill the gaps in your memory of other things, but don't even mention your brother when you're in the same room with me."

And with that she turned and left them.

"Looks like Steven is a popular guy," Maddie said under her breath to Logan when the older woman had gone. "He seems to be more disliked even than I am."

"Makes it kind of tough to find out anything about him when everybody hates him so much they won't even talk about him, doesn't it?" Logan observed, again scanning the room as he seemed wont to do this evening.

"Does that mean we can just dance away the rest of the night and forget about everything else?" she asked hopefully, because in spite of the reason they'd attended this function, she couldn't help yearning for a better way to spend the time.

"We'd be wasting a prime opportunity," he warned. "We aren't likely to get such ready access to so many people who know you and might know Steven."

Of course he was right, but that didn't mean Maddie had to like it, especially not when all she really wanted was to be back in his arms on the dance floor. "Okay, okay. So much for being Cinderella."

"Besides, we did learn something."

"What?"

"That the reason Madeline Van Waltonscot's brother isn't in the will is not because he predeceased her father. It's because he was disinherited—scandalously. So, chances are we're looking for someone who does exist and who has reason to be bugging the heiress for his share of the pot. That increases the odds that the voice on the answering machine is Steven."

"You learned all that just from what little that snobby old lady said? Then I guess we better keep at this."

But they might as well have given up then and there and just enjoyed the evening together. In spite of bringing up Steven Van Waltonscot's name every chance they got, they didn't learn anything about him. Whatever had happened for him to be disinherited had apparently occurred a long time ago, because the mention of his name brought only blank stares, comments about not knowing Madeline had a brother or uncomfortable claims not to have heard anything about him for years. Those few people who had known him also managed to beat hasty retreats immediately after the subject was brought up, as if to escape before anything even more unsavory could be asked of them.

By midnight Maddie and Logan had canvassed the entire ballroom without learning any more than they had from Miriam Prescott Manderlie.

At least not about Steven.

What they had learned was that Madeline Van Waltonscot's acquaintances were not nearly as reluctant to make sly remarks about Logan, to whisper behind their hands that he was her latest amusement, to look right through him or, on a few occasions, to inquire about being next in line for his favors.

It took some of the glamor out of the evening and made both Maddie and Logan anxious for it to end.

"Dance with me one last time and then let's go home," Maddie finally said in exasperation when two women walked by and one of them muttered "gigolo" to the other as they both stole glances at Logan.

"Whatever you say. After all, I am at your service," he joked wryly, even though she knew he'd hated the role so many people had cast him in, and there was nothing he found funny about it.

But as if he'd finished with work and tuned out everything else, for the first time that evening he turned his attention to her alone.

He led her onto the dance floor as the musicians began a slow, sexy song that could have been coming from a 1950s jukebox, and danced with her as if they were the only people left in a dark, smoky bar.

Both of his arms were around her, one palm was high on her bare back, the other so low on her spine his fingertips grazed her rear end.

Maddie smiled up at him, clasping her hands behind his neck and enjoying the audacity of it all as much as his touch.

He didn't lead her through box steps or anything else formal; they just swayed together, from side to side as he held her pressed almost as close to him as they had been in bed the night before.

Maddie didn't know if they were drawing stares from the other guests and she didn't care. She only cared about being there in Logan's arms, looking up at his great face, teasing his chin with the tip of her nose, and fencing with kisses that seemed to land everywhere but on each other's lips as the music carried them along and spun a cocoon around them that blocked out everything and everyone else.

When the song ended he took her hand, and without a moment spared to say good-night to a single soul, he led her out of the ballroom and through the hotel to the lobby.

"I'll get my wrap while you have the car brought up," she told him.

"I don't want you out of my sight," he said in a low, raspy voice for her ears only.

But Maddie knew he wasn't seducing her—at least not solely—he was playing bodyguard, too.

"Nothing's going to happen to me between here and the cloakroom. It's in plain sight of the desk clerk, and there's a hatcheck girl to get the coats, too. Go on," she urged. "We can get home all the sooner."

He hesitated, obviously debating with himself as he glanced around the lobby. But then he squeezed her hand and let go. "Holler if you need me," he instructed, heading out the double glass doors while Maddie went in the other direction, down a hallway directly across the lobby from the reception desk, just as she'd pointed out to Logan.

Apparently they weren't the only guests of the Unessa Ball to call it a night because there was a group of people clustered around the window of the cloakroom.

Not wanting to draw attention to herself and have to talk to more strangers, she hung back, slipping into another, narrower hallway that jutted off to the right and stopping just around the corner so she could keep an eye on the cloakroom and head for it as soon as the other people left.

That was the first time she was aware there had been a man behind her.

He wasn't from the ball, though, because he wore ordinary street clothes—jeans, tennis shoes, a black windbreaker.

A flash of startled fear shot through her at that first glimpse of him, but when she glanced at his face he didn't so much as look her way. Instead he went on past as if he hadn't noticed her. The hallway was a service passage with several doors along the sides marked Employees Only, and from the opposite end were kitchen sounds of pans clattering and dishes banging against one another.

When she realized he must be someone who worked at the hotel, she felt silly and turned back to peeking around the corner at the other guests from the Unessa Ball.

Lord, but they were taking their time.

Hurry up! she urged them in her mind, impatient to end this part of the evening and slip away with Logan, even as she told herself that if she was going to be afraid of anything, it should be how easily and completely she was ignoring her better judgment and letting her heart lead the way with him, as if she were fancy-free instead of in an incredibly bizarre and complicated situation with who knew what hanging over her head.

Playing with fire, that's what she was doing. Playing with—

The hand that shot out from behind her was so quick, so silent that it clamped around her mouth before she was even aware that anyone was there, wrenching her head back at the same moment an arm in a black windbreaker sleeve locked around her waist.

Before she could make more than a squeak, she was pulled through one of the doors into a dark room that smelled of cleaning supplies.

Belatedly she started to struggle, tried to shout, but it didn't matter. Whoever had a hold of her was larger and stronger by far, and before she knew it they were out of that room and into the steamy air of an alley.

But her abductor didn't slow his pace or ease up on his grip even then. He just went on half dragging her, half carrying her, down the alley to the rear of the hotel as Maddie tried hard to break free, to make more than muffled sounds from inside her throat.

One of her shoes came off and then the other, costing her her balance and precious control as her feet slipped out from under her. He completely dragged her from there, and try as she might, she couldn't get back what she'd lost. She was totally at his mercy, hauled like a sack of grain until they reached a white delivery van parked behind a Dumpster.

But even when her captor stopped and she regained her footing, he had a viselike hold of her. He flung the rear doors of the van open. His arm jammed up into her ribcage, knocking the wind out of her as he lifted her and shoved her inside.

Then the doors slammed shut.

And she was sprawled on the van's cold metal floor, gasping for air in pitch-black darkness as the engine started and the wheels shrieked to life.

Chapter Nine

It took Maddie several minutes to catch her breath as the van accelerated and she banged against big rolls of something—carpet, she discovered—on either side of her. When she could breathe again she fought her way to stand up, hit her head on the ceiling and ended on her knees this time, tangled in the length of her gown.

Hanging on to one of the carpet rolls, she yanked her skirt high enough to free her legs. Then she crawled to the rear doors, where a thin slit of light from between them was the only indication that that was the direction she needed to go.

The van careened from side to side, traveling at a high speed and jostling her with every bump in the road, threatening to topple her yet again. It slowed only slightly around corners, the tires screeching their complaint. Still, she decided that if she could get the doors open she could jump out. Anything—broken bones, a concussion, scrapes, scratches—was better than whatever her abductor might have in mind for her. Or maybe another car would be back there and she could get help.

But there were no door handles on the inside. She felt everywhere for them, but they just weren't there.

She tried pushing the doors, anyway, hitting them with her shoulder until it was sore, but nothing worked. She was locked in good and tight, and there wasn't a thing she could do but wait for those doors to be opened from the outside and hope she could make a run for it.

Yet even those hopes were dashed a few moments later when the van slowed, bumped over what felt like a curb and pulled into a garage—if the sudden echo of the engine sounds were any indication. That assumption was confirmed when she heard the whir of a heavy garage door being mechanically lowered.

She wouldn't be able to run for it, she realized with a wave of panic. She wouldn't be able to do anything but face whoever this was who had kidnapped her.

And then the van doors opened.

Once her eyes adjusted to the light, Maddie found herself face-to-face with a man who was clearly an older, wearier version of the high-school graduate in the picture from the ledger. A male rendering of her own new features. Black hair, a slightly long nose, dark blue eyes and a mouth set in an angry, determined line.

"Steven?" Maddie guessed hesitantly.

"Sister, dear," he said facetiously in the voice from the answering machine.

Just then a woman stepped to his side. Maddie judged her to be no taller than she was if they'd been standing shoulder to shoulder, probably ten pounds heavier, with blond hair and wide brown eyes in an oval face. She looked as scared as Maddie felt.

"Get out of the van," Steven ordered.

There were no weapons that Maddie could see, but the force of his anger was enough to keep her wary and doing as he said.

They were indeed in a garage, she found when she climbed down awkwardly. A small one with a door midway along a side wall. The other woman went to that door and unlocked it.

"Go on," Steven ordered again, nodding to the entrance into the house.

Once more Maddie did as she was told—there was nothing else she could do in the cramped space with Madeline Van Waltonscot's brother looming within inches of her and the garage sealing her in. She had to sidestep around the corner of the van to the door where she climbed two simple wooden steps into a very modest home.

Directly across the small combination living room-dining room that she entered was another door.

"Downstairs," Steven barked to Maddie as the other woman opened that door, too, revealing the stairs to a basement.

Maddie didn't budge, knowing her chances of escaping from where she was were better than they would be if she needed to get out of a basement. She turned to Madeline Van Waltonscot's brother, hoping desperately that he'd been disowned by his family and rejected by everyone else for some reason that wouldn't strike out at her and become painfully clear when she disobeyed him.

"I know you're going to find this hard to believe—impossible, maybe," she said as calmly as she could. "But I'm glad to meet ... meet up with you. I'm not exactly sure what's gone on in the past, with Harry Denton or before—the accident blanked out my memory of most things—but I want to make right whatever has gone wrong between you and me."

He just glared at her.

"Steven?" the other woman ventured in a quiet, hopeful voice.

"Don't fall for it, honey. She'll say anything now that she doesn't have that creep Denton to hide behind," he said without taking his eyes off Maddie.

Still, though, she was heartened to hear a gentler tone when he spoke to the woman Maddie assumed to be his wife since they were wearing matching wedding bands.

"If this is about money," Maddie continued, "I'll gladly—"

"I don't want your damn money," he ground out through clenched teeth as if she'd made a mistake to even offer. "Get downstairs."

The tiny amount of fear that had receded when she'd heard him speak to his wife came back now, and when he moved menacingly toward Maddie, she believed he might actually push her down the stairs. It left her no choice but to do his bidding, with him and the other woman following behind.

"To the right," he instructed when she reached the bottom, where a wall separated the basement into two sections—a family room on the left and a laundry room on the right. But when she went in the direction he'd ordered, she found that on the back wall of the laundry room was another door.

"In there," he barked, pointing a long finger at it.

Maddie took a hard swallow. She imagined a small, dark closet and being locked inside of it, held prisoner. Or worse, some kind of torture chamber.

"Please, can't we just sit down and talk? Whatever I've done in the past, I'm not the same person I was then." Although she had no intention of blurting out the details. Instead she tried to explain what had happened since awakening as Madeline Van Waltonscot. "When I began to realize something awful was being done at my request, I even hired another private investigator to find out who was doing it, and to whom and why, so I could stop it all and make up for it."

Steven let out a mirthless chuckle and shook his head in denial. "I hoped that accident might have some positive effect on you. Make you more human. But then Denton started up again, ruining us, and I knew you were just as rotten as before. Just as bad as that old man."

"What old man? Harry Denton? I don't know what you're talking about. But Denton's starting up again when I came out of the coma was his doing from the orders before the accident. I honestly didn't know what was going on until he began to send me anonymous notes about it. Then I had to figure out who he was and find him before I could stop him. But I've done that as of Friday. Nothing else will happen to either of you from here on."

"Yeah, right."

"Please," she repeated. "I really have been looking for you. I found your high-school graduation picture so the investigator and I figured you might be who Denton was harassing, the person who had left those messages on the answering machine. But all we could find when we tried tracking you down was your birth certificate and that didn't lead us anywhere."

"Seems to me Harry Denton would have been happy to share my address with you."

"But that's just it. He wouldn't tell me anything. He was afraid I was trying to double-cross him, so he just denied even knowing me or you or anything about anything. But now that we've connected you could fill me in on so many things I've been wondering about. You could tell me why you aren't a part of my life, why you weren't left half the estate, how I can fix whatever has gone wrong, whatever damage Harry Denton did."

Her plea didn't soften him. "Don't play games with me." He poked his chin toward the door, and his wife opened it the way she had the two before.

But there wasn't a closet on the other side. Or any sort of prison cell or torture chamber. Instead it was a child's room. A little girl's room, if the pink-and-white ruffles over everything were any indication.

Lord, this is even weirder than I thought.

Then Steven shoved her from behind and she bounded into the space.

But she wasn't locked inside. Instead, Madeline Van Waltonscot's brother and his wife came, too.

"Take a look around," he said. "Take a real good look."

Had his voice quavered? Maddie glanced at him, fearing his rage was so great it was pushing him over the edge.

But what she saw was that the rage was only an adjunct to some other emotion. Something much more powerful, much more profound, for there were tears in his eyes. His wife must have seen it, too, because she reached a consoling hand to his arm.

"We had to take Becky to the hospital this morning," he said with accusation in his voice. "She loves this room. I built it for her myself. But she may never get back to it. And all because of you."

Maddie felt cold and clammy. What had the heiress done that a child might not return from a hospital to this room? "I don't know who Becky is," she said very softly, suddenly more afraid of what Madeline Van Waltonscot might have done than of anything else.

"Our daughter, that's who she is!" he shouted as if he thought she'd just forgotten the child's name because it hadn't been important enough for her to remember. "Your niece. Your eight-year-old niece. The little girl who's going to die because of you," he finished through bared teeth.

"Please, pretend I'm a perfect stranger and explain what you're talking about. Honestly, I don't know anything about this."

"Becky has aplastic anemia," the woman explained. "It's a blood disorder. Her bone marrow doesn't make blood cells."

"And you're the only damn person we've been able to find with a blood chemistry that matches hers. The only damn person who can donate bone marrow and save her life."

Maddie's knees felt weak as that news and the logical assumption that the heiress had refused to give that particular donation settled in on her. "Tell me I was going to do it. That the accident just interfered," she said, knowing even as she did that it couldn't be true, remembering Logan saying that Madeline Van Waltonscot had wanted a private investigator to discourage these people from bothering her.

"The only thing the accident interfered with was Harry Denton's troublemaking," Steven spat out.

"You refused even to be tested the first time we asked you," his wife said. "But when we'd done everything else possible to try to find a donor, we had to go back to you. Steven begged you to help us, to put aside everything that had happened in the past, because by then you were our only hope. When you finally agreed to the test we thought ... well, we didn't think you wouldn't go through with the procedure if you really were a match."

Steven interrupted. "Then when you learned what the procedure involved you refused to allow it. You said you didn't like pain or being sick," he sneered.

"But we couldn't find another donor and we were desperate," his wife continued. "There you were, the only person who could save our little girl's life, and you just shrugged it off. We couldn't stop pestering you—"

"*Pestering.* It was only a few phone calls offering you anything you wanted if you'd just help Becky," Steven broke in. "But of course you have everything you want. What could we give you? You said to stop bothering you. *Bothering* you. Our baby is dying and you don't want to be bothered. Instead you hired that creep Harry Denton to ruin us. It wasn't enough that we have a sick child, a child who you're killing by not helping, you didn't even want us in the same state with you, as if we were sullying your air."

Maddie could see that he was at the breaking point, that only his wife's hand on his arm was holding him in check. But she couldn't blame him.

"I prayed ... prayed on my knees," he went on, "that the accident would change your mind. That you would wake up a different person, a person with a conscience, who would ignore a little pain of her own to save our baby. But then Harry Denton started in again and—'' He shook his head as if trying to shake off some of the rage before it exploded. ''I don't know what I thought I'd accomplish by bringing you here tonight. But when I read in the newspaper about that fancy party, I knew you'd go. That you'd be out having a good time while Becky lies in a hospital bed. I just had to do something. I had to get you here, to see that we're people. We have a real life. Becky has toys and dolls and stuffed animals she loves. She has a right to live. To come back here to this room, to her things. To us...''

Steven's voice dwindled off on a pleading note as tears ran down his cheeks.

That was when Maddie realized there were tears running down her face, too. ''It's okay. It's all okay now,'' she said in a near whisper. ''You'll never know just how completely your prayers were answered.''

And so were hers, for at that moment, on silent feet, Logan appeared in the doorway behind Steven.

Maddie thought she was seeing things, but in the blink of an eye he lunged at Madeline Van Waltonscot's brother, grabbing him in a headlock and holding a gun to his temple as Maddie and Steven's wife both shouted, ''No!''

THE SHOWER MADDIE TOOK back at Logan's apartment when they finally got there at three in the morning was long and hot, as if she could wash away what she'd learned about the real Madeline Van Waltonscot. It was bad enough that the heiress had been rude and supercilious, that she'd been a demanding, selfish employer, a petty, mean-spirited excuse for a person. But that she'd also done all she had to her own brother's family after denying help only she could give to an ailing child—well, that boggled Maddie's mind.

And she felt the need to be cleansed in even a small way of the fact that she was now that person.

"You scared the hell out of me tonight, you know?" Logan said when she'd ended her shower, put on the shirt she'd borrowed for warmth after the wedding and went into his bedroom.

He was lying in bed, on pillows propped against the headboard, his broad chest and flat stomach bare above a sheet draped over his lower half.

"It scared the hell out of me, too," she said, climbing into bed, into his arms and settling with her head cushioned on one firm pectoral.

They hadn't been able to exchange more than a few words since Logan had appeared behind Steven. Within moments of that, the place had been filled with police. There had been innumerable questions to answer, and Maddie had had to do a lot of persuading to keep Steven and his wife from being arrested.

Then, when she'd convinced the authorities and Logan to overlook the incident, and Steven and Barb—his wife—that she would meet them at the hospital the next morning for the bone-marrow transplant, she and Logan were driven home by one of the cops, who'd used the time to update Logan on station-house gossip.

But now Maddie could satisfy her curiosity. "How did you find me?"

Logan rubbed feather-light strokes up and down her arm. "I came looking for you after telling the valet to have the car brought up. When you weren't at the cloakroom I knew something was wrong. I could feel it."

"I might have just been in the restroom."

"That was the first place I checked—the one down that service hall."

"You went into the ladies' bathroom yourself?"

"Barged right in, shouting my head off for you. When you weren't there I hit the kitchen and found one of the cops who was supposed to be working security for the ball. The delivery door for the kitchen was open, and just as I was asking if anyone had seen you, the van screeched past. I knew. I just knew you were in it."

"With hunches like these you should be a gambler."

"Cops learn to trust their instincts. Anyway, we ran out into the alley, ran after the van as far as we could, far enough for me to get the license number at least. Then we called in, reported your suspected kidnapping and the plate number so every patrol car would be on the lookout."

"I didn't hear any sirens. No one must have spotted us."

"It was the license number that paid off. Luckily the van belonged to Steven—Wyatt is the last name he's using. When we got the home address from the registration, we headed there. I found a rear window open and used it. Good thing you were inside or I'd have had big explanations to make for that one."

In spite of his attempt to end on a lighter note, Maddie knew that he was still as shaken as she was because his arm was tight around her now, holding her protectively.

"Good work, Former Officer Strummel," she commended like the chief of police to tease him.

Logan didn't say anything for a moment. He just went on holding her, locking both his arms around her and resting his chin on her head.

Maddie could hear the steady beat of his heart, and it helped to ground her. She began to relax, to let the heat of his body infuse hers.

After awhile he said, "So now we know the whole story."

"Mmm. Everything but what happened to make Steven be disowned."

"But we know everything you hired me to find out," he amended. "And tomorrow you'll go in for surgery to give that little girl what she needs to get well."

"I hope it isn't too late. Steven's wife said that having this done earlier would have been better. I can't imagine that Madeline Van Waltonscot refused."

"She was not a nice lady," Logan agreed. "Which, I have no doubt, is why you're here occupying her body instead of her."

"It makes some kind of strange sense, doesn't it? If I had survived the accident in my own body, I probably wouldn't have been a match for the bone-marrow transplant, and the little girl's only hope would have been buried."

"The grand design," Logan mused.

"But is this where it ends?"

"What do you mean?"

"Oh, I don't know. I guess I'm just wondering what happens from here."

"Life goes on?" he suggested.

"Mmm. Madeline Van Waltonscot's life?"

"How about your version of it?"

"My version? You mean rattling around that museum of a house, confusing the staff because I want to make my own coffee and having them drive me nuts by always being around? Or maybe the version where I butt into board meetings and ruin the plans of the powers that be of Scottie's Food Marts? Or the version where I bluff my way—badly—through the heiress's personal relationships? I think I'd rather abdicate the throne and live a simple life of my own."

"Full of blue jeans and hot dogs?"

"Right."

He didn't say anything for a moment, and Maddie had the feeling that he was debating with himself.

Then he took a deep breath and sighed it out. "Nobody wants to encourage you to do that more than me," he admitted.

"I hear a *but* coming."

"But whether you like it or not, you are Madeline Van Waltonscot now. The sad truth is that there isn't a Maggie Morgan anymore. There's also no way of knowing if the grand design involves more than saving Becky Wyatt. Perhaps there are other things you can fix or defend or keep on the up-and-up, or change the course of—like not letting the powers that be at Scottie's Food Marts get away with giving the shaft to a whole slew of employees."

"So abdicating the throne is out?" she said as if he'd dashed her hopes when in fact she knew he was right. She couldn't turn her back on the responsibilities that had come with this second chance to be alive.

But that didn't mean she liked it or was comfortable with it or knew exactly how she was going to fit into the big picture that was Madeline Van Waltonscot's life.

Or how Logan might fit into it.

"I guess there's still a lot to sort through, isn't there?" she said.

"I knew there would be. Quinn and I talked about that exact thing at the wedding."

"Maybe I should hire you to help since you've done pretty well so far," she only half joked, because she couldn't keep from thinking that now that the case was finished, maybe so was their time together, and more than anything she couldn't stand for that to be true.

"You want to put me on the payroll permanently?" he asked in a tone that made it clear he didn't like that idea even in jest.

Maddie knew she'd said exactly the wrong thing. It smacked too much of the way everyone they'd encountered had viewed him—as a gigolo, as the heiress's newest toy, a paid escort whose real duties were all performed behind the bedroom door.

"I didn't mean—"

"I know you didn't." He let silence fall for a few moments and then, as if he sensed what was really on her mind, he said, "I love you, Maddie."

"I love you, too."

"I thought I was going to go crazy tonight when I couldn't find you, when I realized that you were in danger. It opened my eyes to the fact that I don't want to lose you."

"Oh, sure, it takes somebody kidnapping me to open your eyes," she joked again.

But it didn't change his serious tone. "Maybe when you're sorting through all you have to sort through you should add one more thing to the list—marrying me."

"Just maybe? Not for sure?" she asked very softly.

Again some time passed before he answered her. "I've been lying here thinking about what kind of future we might have together. Wondering how I'd handle the role the people around you keep seeing me in. I can't tell you it doesn't bother me, because it does. But it occurred to me that no matter what the world thinks, nothing is as bad as not having you in my life would be, so I decided I'd just deal with it."

But it wouldn't be easy for him. He was a proud man and to be treated the way he had been by the lawyer, the accountant, the people at the ball tonight, would be very hard to accept over the long haul. And they both knew it.

Plus, the fact that he proposed with so much reservation gave Maddie serious pause.

"How would you feel if I was just plain Maggie Morgan?" she asked, testing the waters.

"A lot better," he answered with a laugh. "Then no one would be calling me your gigolo."

But the bottom line was that she wasn't just plain Maggie Morgan.

Nor would she ever be again.

He tipped her chin up with a gentle push of one knuckle and lowered his mouth to hers in a kiss so sweet, so tender it broke her heart.

Or maybe that proposal had.

But there in his arms, at that moment, she didn't want to think the things that were creeping into her mind, she didn't want to have the doubts or the reservations that were suddenly her own. She wanted to escape them all, and the best way to do that was to give herself up to that kiss as it deepened and drew them together, cocooning them against the world, against anything outside of the two of them.

They made love. Passionate love. Poignant love that said more about their feelings for each other than any words.

And at the pinnacle of that act the pure power that was unleashed told Maddie that she loved Logan Strummel in a way she'd never loved anyone.

A way that couldn't bear to accept a proposal that came tied with a ribbon of reservations.

Not that she blamed him as they lay back with their exhausted bodies entwined.

She just couldn't say yes.

Instead, when he asked her to marry him a second time, she didn't say anything at all. She pretended to be asleep.

But long after he was, her eyes were still open.

And she was wishing hard that she were still plain old Maggie Morgan.

Chapter Ten

There was a moment when Maddie woke up from the anesthetic the next day, following the ninety-minute operation that harvested marrow from her hip bones, that she thought she might look under the sheets that covered her and find she'd been returned to her own body. After all, if it could happen once that she opened groggy eyes in a sterile hospital room to find a huge switch had been made while she was unconscious, why couldn't it happen again?

But this time wishing didn't make it so.

Peeking, she found what she'd found that other time—perky breasts, flat stomach, narrow hips, long legs.

She was still Madeline Van Waltonscot.

Which meant she had to go through with what she'd decided before going to sleep the night before.

"Checking to see if all the parts are still there?"

It was Logan's voice that came to her from a chair in the corner of her private hospital room, and as much as the deep rich bass lifted her heart, it caused a crash landing a split second later when she reminded herself of what she had to do.

He stood and came to her bedside, sitting on the edge of the mattress and taking her hand between both of his.

"I was just checking to see if they were the same parts I had before they knocked me out," she told him.

"How do you feel?"

"Okay." There was pain and soreness, but the greater hurt had nothing to do with the surgery.

"You've slept away the whole day. The doctors said your bone marrow has already been cleaned and pumped into Becky Wyatt's bloodstream. She's doing fine and so are you."

Maddie wasn't doing as well as he thought. "Logan," she began, "I want you to know how much I appreciate everything you've done—above and beyond the call of duty—like staying with me today."

He smiled at her, that terrific smile that lightened his whole handsome face, except that there was the shadow of confusion just behind it. "That sounds pretty formal. And what was it you said last night? Do I hear a *but* coming?"

"I want to talk about your marriage proposal." She slipped her hand from between his and had to let her eyes drift closed for a moment as the anesthetic and the effects of the surgery tried to put her back to sleep.

But she fought it and forced her lids open again to see the sober expression on Logan's face, which said he realized that what she'd just said wasn't a good sign.

"You're supposed to think about marrying me while you sort through where you're going from here," he reminded.

"I've thought about it all I need to."

"Ah, Maddie..." He grimaced. "I know my proposal probably seemed halfhearted to you last night. I'm sorry for that. But it'll be okay. I've had a lot of time to think today while you've slept, and I really do know without a doubt that nothing else matters as much as having you in my life."

"Except that I wouldn't only be in your life, you'd have to be in mine, too. In Madeline Van Waltonscot's."

"I'll deal with it."

But it was too late for her to feel confident about that when she'd already seen his doubts so clearly.

"Marriage is a tough proposition," she said, hearing the thickness in her own voice and finding the battle with fatigue more difficult to fight. "This bizarre situation is hard to fathom, harder still to get used to, to deal with. Marrying into it... Well, I just think that that's double jeopardy. And when it isn't something you can do freely and without the slightest qualm..."

"I wouldn't be human if I hadn't had the slightest qualm."

"I know." She swallowed and tried to wet her dry lips with her tongue. "But don't you see, there's enough for me to deal with without your not being completely committed."

That made him mad. "Who said I'm not completely committed? Do you think I proposed to you on a lark?"

"Maybe that wasn't a good choice of words."

"Maybe we shouldn't be talking about this when you're still half out of it."

"I'm not half out of it. Just really tired. Besides, I made this decision before the surgery."

"Which explains why you were so quiet on the way here."

"I love you, Logan," she said softly. "But I'm too unsure of where I'm going, of what's in store for me as Madeline Van Waltonscot or how I'll deal with it all. How can I add a marriage that throws your uncertainties into the mix? I'm not saying you aren't right. You'd be crazy not to have second thoughts about putting yourself in a position to be treated forever the way you have been. I'm just saying that when someone has doubts, any doubts, that isn't the time to get married."

"I don't have doubts anymore, Maddie. And the doubts were never about you and me. About my feelings for you or yours for me. About wanting to spend the rest of my life with you. They were about outside influences. But the more I thought about it today, the more I thought to hell with those outside influences. The lawyer, the accountant, the whole damn city can believe I'm a gigolo for all I care. The only thing that's important is that we're together."

But just the night before he wasn't feeling that way, and Maddie couldn't forget that. She shook her head but it took an incredible amount of effort to do it. "It won't work, Logan," she said with pain-filled finality.

"It won't if you won't let it," he shot out. Then he took a breath, sighed and visibly calmed himself. "Damn it, Maddie, I love you and that's all that should matter."

"Maybe it's all that should matter, but it isn't all that does. It also matters that you can't go into the marriage freely, without concerns, without sacrificing your pride, without hating that you'd have to be the brunt of ugly whispers. That matters to you, and I just don't believe that was wiped out because you thought a little more about it. Or that it won't matter again the next time it happens."

He stood and stared down at her—glared down at her, actually. "There's nothing I can do or say except what I have. I love you. I'm willing to deal with the down side of being married to you so I can have the up side—you."

"But don't you see? There shouldn't be a down side."

"Maddie..."

Terrible, terrible weariness washed over her. "Our being together just wasn't part of the grand design," she said softly, closing her eyes against the hot tears that suddenly stung them. "If it had been, it wouldn't come at the expense of your pride. It wouldn't be something that came with so much to overlook in order for it to happen."

"You're wrong. You're so damn wrong," he said too loudly for a hospital.

"I'm not wrong," she whispered, sure that she wasn't, regardless of how much it hurt.

"You know, if you weren't lying in that bed, sick, I'd shake some damn sense into you."

"It wouldn't change anything," she insisted stubbornly, opening her eyes again. "You're nobody's boy toy and you shouldn't have to be treated like you are. And when you get married—" Her voice cracked at the thought that when he did, it wouldn't be to her, but she forced herself past it. "And when you get married, you should be able to do it without any reservations."

"You're tired. You need to rest. I'll come back tomorrow and we'll hash this out," he said reasonably.

"Yes, I'm tired and I need to rest. But don't come back, Logan. I won't change my mind."

"Damn it, Maddie—"

"Go. Please just go."

She shut her eyes yet again, but she knew he stayed standing there for a few minutes more, and a part of her wanted him to say or do something that could convince her she was wrong, even when she knew she wasn't.

But then she heard the door open and close, and even without looking she knew he'd gone.

She knew it by the emptiness he left behind.

In the room.

And in her heart.

MADDIE HAD BEEN HOME from the hospital for two days when Bernice knocked on her sitting-room door to say she had a visitor.

"Logan?" she asked in hope-filled reflex.

"I'm sorry, no. He gave his name as Steven."

Embarrassed to have shown so much of her wish that the single visitor would be Logan, and fighting the horrible disappointment that it wasn't, Maddie forced a smile, however wan. "Oh. That's a surprise." Just not the one she'd have preferred. And also not one she was completely comfortable with, so she said, "I'll see him downstairs."

The personal assistant looked skeptical. Maddie's recuperation had kept her in her rooms on the third floor because stiffness and soreness made all those steps no easy task.

"It's okay," she answered the other woman's expression. "I'll just take it slowly."

"Shall I help you?"

"No, thanks. It's not that bad."

It wasn't that good, either. But Maddie finally made it about ten minutes later, finding Steven standing stiffly in the foyer waiting for her.

He grimaced as if he were feeling the pain as he watched her descend the last few steps, and rather than greeting him, Maddie ended up assuring him, too, that it was no big deal.

"Come on, let's sit in the living room," she suggested, leading the way and easing herself onto one of the stuffy couches just before glancing back at him and catching his disbelieving look at what she was wearing.

Not the elaborate peignoir set he expected, she thought. Instead she had on a plain navy-blue sweatsuit that had been an anonymous gift the day she was set to leave the hospital.

She had no doubt it was from Logan, and somehow every time she put it on it not only aided her physical comfort but made her feel connected to him—a double-edged sword that both hurt and helped the much bigger emotional wound she'd been trying to cure since sending him away after the surgery.

"How's Becky?" she asked when Steven had rejected her offer of something to eat or drink and sat on a Queen Anne chair across from her.

"She's doing really well. Her white-blood-cell count is better every day, which means she's recovering. Thanks to you," he added a bit gruffly, obviously feeling awkward.

Maddie wasn't sure how to put him at ease, with all the water that had gone under the bridge between Steven and his sister before the accident. It seemed like too great a task to be accomplished in only a few words. So she just said, "If there's anything else I can do, anything at all—"

"I'm not only here about Becky," he interrupted, crossing one jean-clad calf over the opposite knee and hanging on to it as if he were trying to appear more relaxed than he was. "Your lawyer contacted me yesterday. I have to tell you I was shocked to hear that you're giving me a full half of the inheritance. I never expected or even thought about that happening, but this is all the more of a surprise seeing as how the first thing you said to me when I came to ask you to help Becky was that I was no longer a Van Waltonscot and might as well not even think about getting my mitts on any of your money."

It was Maddie's turn to grimace. "I know you don't believe me, but I really am not the same person I was before," she said, although she'd decided never again to confide the truth of the body switch to anyone for fear of being thought crazy enough to lock up. "I barely remember what I was like then."

"Or how you felt about things?"

"Yes, or how I felt about things. And when I finally had all the pieces of the puzzle put together about who you are, I just didn't see any reason why you shouldn't have what rightfully belongs to you."

He studied her for a moment through eyes the same dark blue as her own. "You really don't remember, do you?"

"Virtually nothing. Including why you were disowned in the first place. But I am curious about it."

"You don't even have a faint hint of a memory about the beatings?"

"Beatings?" she repeated with quiet horror. "No, I don't remember anything about that."

"Do you remember the old man at all?"

She remembered Steven making a comment about an old man the night he'd kidnapped her. She'd thought he might be referring to Harry Denton. Now she realized he must mean his father. "I've seen pictures around here of both Mom and Dad, but no, I don't have any more memory of them than I do of you."

"*Mom and Dad?* We never called them that. It was always *Mother and Father.*"

"Whoops. Told you I don't remember much."

Something about that made Steven chuckle slightly. "It's probably a blessing that you don't remember dear old dad, anyway, the bastard."

"He was the abuser?"

"Abuser seems like such a mild word for what he was. Ritual torture, that's what he dished out. For sport. He'd walk into the room, put on those leather driving gloves to protect his hands, and then talk about what he was going to do before he even did it. He liked to watch the fear mount. He also liked to lay out his trumped-up reasons for the beating. He was always making a man out of me or teaching me a lesson." Steven paused a moment. "You really don't remember?"

She shook her head. "None of it."

"Well, he didn't beat you—at least he didn't while I was living here, I don't know about after I left. But I doubt it. He used to say the two of you were like peas in a pod, that you were his treasure. But you knew about what he did to me, to Mother."

"I don't know now. How long did this go on?"

"For me? Until I was about fourteen. And don't ask me why it stopped then because I was never privy to the reason. Maybe it was because I reached a point where I wouldn't beg him not to do it anymore. No matter what he dished out, I just took it. I refused to show pain, to show fear, to show anything. Maybe it took the fun out of it for him. But he still went after Mother. And listening to it was as bad as getting it myself."

He paused, shook his head, frowned so deeply it looked like it hurt.

Then he went on. "I can't tell you how impotent it made me feel to hear him hurting her and not to be able to do anything about it, to be so paralyzed by fear that I couldn't find the strength to help her. And the older I got the worse it was, the more I tried to convince myself that she could end the beatings the way I did, if she'd just quit begging, quit crying, quit—" Steven jammed his hand through his hair and bit off the rest of what he was going to say.

He drew a deep breath and sighed it out. "I've been through therapy. I know all the emotions were—are normal under the circumstances."

"I still don't understand why you were disinherited. Was it to punish you for robbing him of his fun?"

"No. The night after my graduation I came home from a party to the sounds of him going at Mother worse than I'd ever heard before and I just snapped. He had her locked in their rooms, and even though I tried I couldn't break down the door—it isn't as easy as it looks in the movies. Although it's probably a good thing because if I'd have gotten in there I might have killed him.''

"So what did you do?"

"I called the cops."

"No one had done that before? There's always someone around here—"

"Not then there wasn't. He planned the beatings. He'd send all the staff away for the night—actually that was part of the ritual. He'd announce over dinner that as soon as the meal was cleared everyone was getting an impromptu evening off, and then we'd know what was coming. And as for any neighbors hearing, the house sits too far away from everything.''

"What about bruises or broken bones? Didn't anyone end up needing medical attention after abuse like that?"

"Sure. Most of the time. He just called his private physician and paid him enough not to report anything.''

"And he didn't like that you called in the police the night of your graduation."

"No, he didn't. Not that my calling the cops helped in the way I'd always fantasized it would, though. He bribed the police so no charges were filed. He just bought himself out of it. But I'd embarrassed him. Word leaked to his social circle, there was talk.''

"And that was why he disowned you," Maddie guessed.

"Disowned, disinherited and banned me from having any contact with you or Mother ever again.''

"But Mother saw you, anyway, on the sly, and gave you money."

"You do remember some things. She couldn't risk seeing me too often. If he'd have caught her..." Steven took a deep breath and just shook his head rather than finishing that. "Yes, she tried to help me financially, too, even though I was terrified the money would be what he found out about."

"And then she died and you stopped having any contact with the family at all," Maddie guessed again, filling in details that were obvious.

"I hadn't seen you, anyway. You were so close to him, so much like him. We couldn't risk that you'd tell him what Mother was doing. And I don't think you really wanted to see me. You liked being an only child," he said pointedly, frowning at her as if recalling all of this made it more difficult to believe she really was different now.

"But then Becky got sick and you had to come to me," Maddie concluded to distract him.

He fidgeted slightly and skipped from there back to the subject that had begun all of this. "The last thing I expected was for you to share the estate—then or now. And I have to tell you, I'm wondering why."

"It just seemed like the right thing to do." After thinking about it, Maddie had decided that keeping Madeline Van Waltonscot's half was part and parcel of what came along with the body switch, but she could never have kept Steven's portion, too. That would have felt like stealing from him.

"The right thing to do." He chuckled once more and shook his head. "You are different."

"What I'd like is to put the past behind us. Maybe start over fresh. Could we do that?"

He was staring at her again, his brow furrowed. "I don't know. I guess we could try. I really don't know what to make of you now."

"That's okay. I don't quite know what to make of me, either." Then she changed the subject again. "You know, part of the inheritance includes this house. And it's so huge, if you wanted to bring your family here—"

He laughed ironically at that. Then he glanced around the place and apologized. "I know this is your home and that was classless of me, but the idea of Barb and Becky and me in this mausoleum— I'm sorry, I shouldn't have said that, either."

"It's all right," Maddie assured him with a smile of her own. It was good to know she wasn't the only one who thought of the house that way. "I just want to be sure you know that you really are entitled to half of everything. And I hope it helps make up for all the ugliness with Harry Denton and not doing what should have been done for Becky before."

"Becky's on the mend, so that's all that matters. And as for the rest, yeah, making me a wealthy man makes up pretty well for costing Barb her receptionist's job and me my real-estate license. I don't think I'll have to go back to laying carpet the way I'd planned."

"But you're sure you don't want to live here?"

He looked around again, spotted Bernice peeking at them and grinned to himself. "I could never go back to living like this. No watching football in my underwear. No hearing Becky make a ruckus in her room. No smelling Barb's brownies baking. No thanks. We'll probably get a new house, bigger than what we have, and we'll definitely buy new cars, probably take Becky to Disneyland when she's ready. But on the whole, we won't live a lot differently than we have. I'm pretty happy with things the way they are."

"What about Scottie's Food Marts? You own half of all that now, which means you have a say in everything on the business end, too."

"I know, the lawyer told me. I suppose I'll have to go to board meetings and pay some attention to that, but it's all worked without me for this long. I can't see where it needs much of me in the future."

He stood to go and Maddie pushed herself to her feet, too.

"Would it be okay if I went to visit Becky in the hospital?"

"Sure. I don't know why not. She really liked you when you met up there before. She says you tell great stories."

Maddie laughed. "Yeah, I'm having to get real good at it," she said more to herself than to him. "And maybe you and Barb and I could have dinner sometime?"

He seemed to consider that before he agreed. "I'll call you."

Maddie wasn't sure if he meant that, and yet she was grateful just to have the hope that at some point she might actually have people in her life who didn't work for her.

She walked him to the front door.

"What about you?" he asked along the way. "You seemed pretty close to that P.I. who showed up the other night. If we have dinner would he be coming?"

That idea, and the extent to which she wished it could be, stabbed her. "We aren't seeing each other now," she answered very softly.

"I'm sorry if that was out of line. It just seemed like there was something personal between the two of you."

"You weren't out of line, you were right. There was something personal between us. It's just that there isn't anymore." And admitting that out loud nearly did her in.

Once again Steven glanced around and shook his head. "Must get lonely here," he said, and this time it was Steven who seemed to be talking more to himself than to her. She also had the sense that he wasn't referring only to the house, but to her life and how different it was from his.

Or maybe that was just how she saw it. How she had seen it since Logan had made that same observation.

Then Steven seemed to shake off whatever it was that had been going through his mind, promised to call her and left.

And to Maddie the sound of the front door closing after him echoed even more than usual.

She envied Madeline Van Waltonscot's brother. He was going back to his family, to people who loved him, to a normal life. Oh, what she wouldn't give to be in his shoes, to be with Logan.

A huge wave of that loneliness he'd pinpointed washed over her, and she sank down onto one of the two chairs that stood like sentries on either side of the front door, looking around the foyer, up the stairs, at the chandelier, into the rooms she could see from there.

It had been so easy for Steven to say no to this place. To accept his portion of the Van Waltonscot estate on his own terms. He hadn't even seemed to consider allowing it to alter his life in any way he didn't want it to.

And that was when Logan's words from the last night they'd been together came back to her.

She could live her own version of Madeline Van Waltonscot's life, he'd said.

And suddenly she asked herself why she couldn't do just that. Steven was. And if Steven could reject living here in favor of what it was he wanted for himself, why couldn't she?

Light dawned inside of her. She sat up straighter and considered her future from a new perspective.

She wasn't imprisoned in Madeline Van Waltonscot's life, only in her body. Sure, there might be responsibilities attached to that body, but just as Steven was accepting responsibilities along with his share of the inheritance, without altering the way he lived, her portion of those responsibilities didn't have to be met in the way they'd always been met before, either.

Couldn't she do what she felt to be her part in being a watchdog over Scottie's Food Marts without living the pampered, overly formal Van Waltonscot life-style?

Couldn't she continue to make whatever charitable donations the heiress made without attending snooty balls where other heiresses treated Logan like a toy that could be passed around?

Wasn't she free to change whatever she wanted, just the same as she'd changed the refusal to be the bone-marrow donor and the exclusion of Steven from the will?

Of course she was.

She didn't need to pretend to be the heiress. She *was* the heiress. Who *she* was who Madeline Van Waltonscot was now. Whatever she did, however she behaved, however she chose to live was Madeline Van

Waltonscot's life. With the trappings and all the people who had put down Logan, or without the trappings and all the people who had put down Logan.

And if what she chose was to lead a more down-to-earth life that didn't include the snobs who were in place in it already, wouldn't that also mean that Logan wouldn't be put in the position he'd been in? The position that had caused him to have reservations about a future with her?

It did.

And if it did, there wasn't any reason she could see that she and Logan couldn't be together.

Unless, of course, his reservations hadn't been only about the role of gigolo that those people had cast him in.

What if his qualms had been about getting married in general? Or about her?

But her own moment of doubt was fleeting.

Logan was not the kind of man to propose unless he honestly wanted her to be his wife. Any more than he was the kind of man to say one thing bothered him when really something else did.

And as for his having reservations about her personally?

That was silly. She knew he'd accepted that she was only Madeline Van Waltonscot on the outside, that he didn't question who and what she actually was on the inside. And she also knew he loved her for that inside.

She knew one other thing, as she sat in that foyer. She knew she loved Logan. Too much to live any life without him.

"Whoever can hear me, would you show yourself, please?" she said out loud.

Instantly Bernice stepped from the office door down the hallway alongside the staircase, two maids came front and center from the living room she'd just left and the houseman appeared on the second-floor landing.

They really did come out of the woodwork around here, she thought with amusement now. "Could one of you have the car brought around? There's someplace I need to go. Right away."

IT TOOK MADDIE a little over an hour to find Logan. He wasn't at the carriage-house apartment or at the office of Strummel Investigations. But Lindsey had been there and had told her he was on a surveillance, and where.

Maddie supposed it didn't help him to be unobtrusive when the long white limousine pulled up beside his Jeep and she got out, but she just couldn't wait indefinitely for him to finish this job. Instead she made the transfer from the limo to the Jeep as quickly as she could and sent the chauffeur on his way.

"Hi," she said simply to Logan's wide-eyed, arched-brow stare.

"Hi," he answered tentatively.

"Remember me? Interior decorator reincarnated as heiress?"

"I have a vague recollection."

"Only a vague one? I'd have thought I was pretty memorable."

"What are you doing here, Maddie?

She assumed he meant *besides* struggling with nervousness and worry that he'd say *Scram, lady, you had your chance and blew it.* "I thought I'd come fill you in on the last piece of the Van Waltonscot puzzle.''

"You should be home resting.''

"This couldn't wait. Steven came to see me a while ago,'' she began as if that was the only reason she'd come, going on to explain what had happened to cause the heiress's brother to be disowned.

"Very interesting,'' Logan said disinterestedly when she'd finished. "So why are you really here?''

"Well,'' she answered matter-of-factly, "after Steven left I got to thinking about him and what his portion of the Van Waltonscot fortune was and wasn't going to change for him, and about your idea that I could have my own version of Madeline Van Waltonscot's life, and I realized that I can put my two cents' worth in on the business to keep it fair and honest, I can donate to charities, but I don't have to do any of it from that museum of a house or all dressed up every minute, or among a bunch of snobby, rude people who can't recognize true love when they see it.''

"True love.''

"It is true love, isn't it? You weren't just leading me on because you have a thing for people who've come back from the brink of death into a body they weren't born with the first time around, were you?''

"Well, it might have started out that way,'' he deadpanned. "But it turned into true love later on.''

"Good, because I was thinking that if we didn't hang around with those snooty people who thought you were my boy toy, that maybe you wouldn't have any reservations about marrying me and then I wouldn't have any reservations about your reservations and—''

"And we could get married.''

"And live like regular people."

He hadn't taken his eyes off her since she'd gotten into the Jeep, but that was the first time he smiled at her. "So you got out of a sickbed in a mansion to show up in a limo where I'm sitting spying on a suspected insurance defrauder to ask me to marry you and live like regular people?" he summarized wryly.

"That's about it. I figure changing my name to Maddie Strummel will finally give me my own identity. Oh, and I love you. There is that, too."

"Oh, and I love you. There is that, too," he answered in the same teasing voice.

"So what do you say. Any reservations about marrying me now?"

"None. But then I tried to tell you that I didn't have any when you were in the hospital. And I was biding my time until I thought you felt better and might have come to grips with just who you are before I paid you a little visit to tell you again. More forcefully, if that's what it took."

"So you weren't just going to accept my rejection?" she asked, delighted to hear it.

"No, I wasn't. But this whole thing could have been avoided if you had just listened to me before."

"So shoot me for not thinking straight. I was a couple of quarts low on bone marrow then. What did you expect?"

He reached over and clasped the back of her neck. "All things considered, I'd rather kiss you than shoot you, if that's all right," he said as he pulled her nearer and did just that.

"Besides," he went on when he let her up for air a moment later, "if I shoot you, you'd probably just come back as someone else and we'd have to figure out why and this whole thing would start over again."

"And it might not be in a designer body the next time."

He gave her the once-over and laughed. "Not that anyone can tell that it's a designer body in that sweat suit."

"Thanks for it, anyway."

"You knew it was from me?"

"Who else cares enough?"

His smile this time was soft. "I do love you, you know?" he said much more seriously.

"Good, because I love you, too. And there's nothing I want to be more than your wife."

"Which is part of the grand design."

"So."

He kissed her again, longer, deeper, in a way that sealed their commitment to each other.

Then he started the Jeep's engine. "Now let's get you home."

"Your home?"

"Do you think I'm going to take you where a bunch of other people can butt in and keep me from taking care of you myself?"

"I hope not," she said, laying her head on his broad shoulder as he pulled away from the curb.

This really was part of the grand design, Maddie thought as she closed her eyes and breathed in the scent of his after-shave, and finally, truly, relaxed.

Yes, she might have been sent into Madeline Van Waltonscot's body to save Becky Wyatt. Yes, she might have been sent to help the people employed by Scottie's Food Marts. Yes, she might have been sent to give Steven what he rightfully deserved.

But finding Logan, falling in love with him, having a future with him, those were all a part of that grand design, too. She could feel it. Feel how right it was. Feel how right it would always be.

And for that, for him, she offered up a great big prayer of thanks.

Once in a while, there's a story so special, a story so unusual, that your pulse races, your blood rushes. We call this

HART'S DREAM is one such story.

At first they were dreams—strangely erotic. Then visions—strikingly real. Ever since his accident, when Dr. Sara Carr's sweet voice was his only lifeline, Daniel Hart couldn't get the woman off his mind. Months later it was more than a figment of his imagination calling to him, luring him, doing things to him that only a flesh-and-blood woman could.... But Sara was nowhere to be found....

#589 HART'S DREAM
by
Mary Anne Wilson

Available in July wherever Harlequin books are sold. Watch for more Heartbeat stories, coming your way—only from American Romance!

IT'S A BABY BOOM!

NEW ARRIVALS

We're expecting—again! Join us for a reprisal of the New Arrivals promotion, in which special American Romance authors invite you to read about equally special heroines—all of whom are on a nine-month adventure! We expect each mom-to-be will find the man of her dreams—and a daddy in the bargain!

Watch for the newest arrival!

#600 ANGEL'S BABY
by Pamela Browning
September 1995

PRIZE SURPRISE SWEEPSTAKES!

This month's prize:

BEAUTIFUL WEDGWOOD CHINA!

This month, as a special surprise, we're giving away a bone china dinner service for eight by Wedgwood**, one of England's most prestigious manufacturers!

Think how beautiful your table will look, set with lovely Wedgwood china in the casual Countryware pattern! Each five-piece place setting includes dinner plate, salad plate, soup bowl and cup and saucer.

The facing page contains two Entry Coupons (as does every book you received this shipment). Complete and return *all* the entry coupons; **the more times you enter, the better your chances of winning!**

Then keep your fingers crossed, because you'll find out by September 15, 1995 if you're the winner!

Remember: The more times you enter, the better your chances of winning!*

PRIZE SURPRISE
SWEEPSTAKES

OFFICIAL ENTRY COUPON

This entry must be received by: AUGUST 30, 1995
This month's winner will be notified by: SEPTEMBER 15, 1995

YES, I want to win the Wedgwood china service for eight! Please enter me in
the drawing and let me know if I've won!

Name_____

Address _____ Apt. _____

City   State/Prov.   Zip/Postal Code

Account #_____

Return entry with invoice in reply envelope.

© 1995 HARLEQUIN ENTERPRISES LTD.   CWW KAL

PRIZE SURPRISE
SWEEPSTAKES

OFFICIAL ENTRY COUPON

This entry must be received by: AUGUST 30, 1995
This month's winner will be notified by: SEPTEMBER 15, 1995

YES, I want to win the Wedgwood china service for eight! Please enter me in
the drawing and let me know if I've won!

Name_____

Address _____ Apt. _____

City   State/Prov.   Zip/Postal Code

Account #_____

Return entry with invoice in reply envelope.

© 1995 HARLEQUIN ENTERPRISES LTD.   CWW KAL

OFFICIAL RULES
PRIZE SURPRISE SWEEPSTAKES 3448
NO PURCHASE OR OBLIGATION NECESSARY

Three Harlequin Reader Service 1995 shipments will contain respectively, coupons for entry into three different prize drawings, one for a Panasonic 31" wide-screen TV, another for a 5-piece Wedgwood china service for eight and the third for a Sharp ViewCam camcorder. To enter any drawing using an Entry Coupon, simply complete and mail according to directions.

There is no obligation to continue using the Reader Service to enter and be eligible for any prize drawing. You may also enter by hand printing the words "Prize Surprise," your name and address on a 3"x5" card and the name of the prize you wish that entry to be considered for (i.e., Panasonic wide-screen TV, Wedgwood china or Sharp ViewCam). Send your 3"x5" entries via first-class mail (limit: one per envelope) to: Prize Surprise Sweepstakes 3448, c/o the prize you wish that entry to be considered for, P.O. Box 1315, Buffalo, NY 14269-1315, USA or P.O. Box 610, Fort Erie, Ontario L2A 5X3, Canada.

To be eligible for the Panasonic wide-screen TV, entries must be received by 6/30/95; for the Wedgwood china, 8/30/95; and for the Sharp ViewCam, 10/30/95.

Winners will be determined in random drawings conducted under the supervision of D.L. Blair, Inc., an independent judging organization whose decisions are final, from among all eligible entries received for that drawing. Approximate prize values are as follows: Panasonic wide-screen TV ($1,800); Wedgwood china ($840) and Sharp ViewCam ($2,000). Sweepstakes open to residents of the U.S. (except Puerto Rico) and Canada, 18 years of age or older. Employees and immediate family members of Harlequin Enterprises, Ltd., D.L. Blair, Inc., their affiliates, subsidiaries and all other agencies, entities and persons connected with the use, marketing or conduct of this sweepstakes are not eligible. Odds of winning a prize are dependent upon the number of eligible entries received for that drawing. Prize drawing and winner notification for each drawing will occur no later than 15 days after deadline for entry eligibility for that drawing. Limit: one prize to an individual, family or organization. All applicable laws and regulations apply. Sweepstakes offer void wherever prohibited by law. Any litigation within the province of Quebec respecting the conduct and awarding of the prizes in this sweepstakes must be submitted to the Regies des loteries et Courses du Quebec. In order to win a prize, residents of Canada will be required to correctly answer a time-limited arithmetical skill-testing question. Value of prizes are in U.S. currency.

Winners will be obligated to sign and return an Affidavit of Eligibility within 30 days of notification. In the event of noncompliance within this time period, prize may not be awarded. If any prize or prize notification is returned as undeliverable, that prize will not be awarded. By acceptance of a prize, winner consents to use of his/her name, photograph or other likeness for purposes of advertising, trade and promotion on behalf of Harlequin Enterprises, Ltd., without further compensation, unless prohibited by law.

For the names of prizewinners (available after 12/31/95), send a self-addressed, stamped envelope to: Prize Surprise Sweepstakes 3448 Winners, P.O. Box 4200, Blair, NE 68009.

RPZ KAL